Lights, Latkes, *and* Love

PEGGY BIRD
author of *Sparked by Love* and *Unmasking Love*

Crimson Romance
New York   London   Toronto   Sydney   New Delhi

CRIMSON
ROMANCE

Crimson Romance
An Imprint of Simon & Schuster, Inc.
1230 Avenue of the Americas
New York, NY 10020

For information about special discounts for bulk purchases, please contact Simon & Schuster Special Sales at 1-866-506-1949 or business@simonandschuster.com.

The Simon & Schuster Speakers Bureau can bring authors to your live event. For more information or to book an event contact the Simon & Schuster Speakers Bureau at 1-866-248-3049 or visit our website at www.simonspeakers.com.

ISBN: 978-1-4405-8793-1
ISBN: 978-1-4405-8794-8 (ebook)

For Max, who really did say that to a barista once, and for Meg, who refused to wear burning candles on her head. Thank you for letting me mine your lives for my writing. (And thank you, Meg, for that description.)

Chapter 1

"I *hate* the public. Hate, hate, hate the public." Hannah Jenkins spit out the words as she flopped into an overstuffed chair and waved away the glass of wine her housemate Sarah offered.

"Really? The entire public? Worldwide? Or just Portland, Oregon, and its environs?" Sarah accompanied her question with an exaggerated eye roll.

"Okay, maybe not *all* the public. Just the ones who're a pain in the butt this time of year. Which, face it, is a large number."

"Sure you won't have a glass of wine? It might take the edge off your pissed-offness."

"If I start drinking tonight, I might never stop until the damn Christmas season is over. Which is weeks away. By then, I'd do in my liver and my tombstone would read, 'She was right: Christmas killed her.'"

Hannah was the manager of the flagship—and largest—store in a chain of women's specialty shops. She'd worked her way up from part-time clerk to sales associate to buyer and now to store manager, all by the age of thirty-two, an impressive accomplishment. She loved working in the heart of the city. Loved her colleagues. Loved everything about working retail.

Except Christmas. She hated Christmas.

Sarah settled on the couch and took a sip of her wine. "Maybe if you vent, you'll be in a better mood for the dinner I've spent the last hour preparing. So, tell me, what happened today?"

Hannah knew her housemate was asking only because she was a good friend. Sarah had heard this particular rant each year at this time ever since they'd moved in together.

"Not everyone was an asshat," Hannah admitted, "but there were enough to prove that the idea that everyone has a generous holiday spirit is a huge lie."

Peggy Bird

"Specifics, please," Sarah said with an annoying grin. "You know me. I don't like generalities."

"Okay, there was this jerk who spent a boatload of money on a miniscule bit of lace the manufacturer calls a 'nightgown.' For his girlfriend, he said."

"What's so bad about that?"

Hannah snorted. "He also bought a pair of bunny slippers and a flannel nightgown for his wife and a second nightgown for his secretary—who, I'm sure, does more than print out his schedule for him."

"Oh."

Hannah was almost happy to see her housemate's disappointed slouch. "After him was the woman who thought she could bargain with me for the last bottle of 'Tragic' perfume in the entire city. Telling me that since it was the last one, we couldn't advertise it, so I might as well let her take it off my hands. Like I'm gonna give her a break on the price of the hottest scent to come along since Chanel No. 5. She was so pissed off she filled out an official complaint form saying I wasn't living up to the store's customer-friendly reputation." By now Hannah was sitting with her spine in military alignment, her chin jutting out and her hands in fists.

"But the topper was the woman who said her two teacup poodles were service dogs, so we couldn't ask her to leave them outside. She asked one of my sales staff to hold them while she tried on a half-dozen dresses. Said she was looking for something special for her Christmas-card picture. When she finally decided on one she liked, she grabbed the stupid dogs back to see how they looked with what she'd chosen, and one of the little furballs peed all over the five-hundred-dollar dress, which the woman then refused to buy."

"Don't get angry at the dog. It's not his ... her ... fault."

"I'll apologize to the dog if I ever see it again. But damn it—"

5

"I get it. Bad day at the office." Sarah waved her hand at the bottle on the table. "A bit of the grape might make you feel better about it. Are you sure you won't join me?"

"Maybe I will." Hannah pulled herself out of the depths of the chair and poured a small glass of wine. "I swear, if this job wasn't the best I've ever had, I'd quit. Or at least take a leave until January."

If she were honest about it, Hannah would have to admit she didn't hate everything about working retail during the holidays. For example, she loved the profits. And she didn't object to some of what went along with the season, like the background music that played endlessly from Thanksgiving through Christmas Eve. Didn't even mind having to put up the glittery decorations the night before Thanksgiving so the store was ready to greet shoppers on Black Friday.

It was what happened beginning on Black Friday that she hated—people showed up to shop. There was the crux of her problem. She was ashamed to admit to anyone except her roommate that nasty, stressed, badly behaving customers were the reason she'd come to hate the entire Christmas season. No one seemed to be happy this time of the year. At least not that she noticed. People came into her store, made demands, treated her staff badly, and killed any sense of joy by behaving like—well, like toddlers who hadn't napped in a week. Or kindergartners deprived of their afternoon snacks. Or infants who'd lost their pacifiers.

Sadly, those pathetic examples of Christmas cheer she'd just vented about to Sarah were only the tip of the iceberg. She hadn't even mentioned the shoplifters and credit-card scammers or the people who deliberately damaged merchandise to try and get a discount. Sure, they were around the rest of the year, but the holidays brought more of them out of the woodwork.

Hannah had tried to tell herself that, as manager, she only had to deal with the customers who were difficult, and didn't see the nice people who were there every day. Tried to believe that not everyone was a PITA. But the closer it got to Christmas, the more difficult it was to believe when all she ever saw was a long line of belligerent people like the teacup poodle woman. And all her staff gossiped about were people like the man who'd involved her store in his cheating ways.

If this was what the holiday spirit was about, she wanted none of it.

Which was sad because when she was younger, she'd loved Christmas—the food, the presents, the anticipation, the lights. She especially loved the lights. She'd grown up on Peacock Lane, a four-block-long street in southeast Portland known for its Christmas-light displays. Every house on the lane was a glowing celebration of the season. Trees, bushes, rooflines, doors—everything that could support lights was draped in them. When it was lit up for its annual celebration of the season, the street was visible from the international space station, her father used to tell her. She believed him until she was a lot older than she liked to admit.

Hannah couldn't pinpoint the exact moment her enjoyment of the season had begun to wane. It could have been the year her family's beautiful light display, along with several others on the street, was damaged by vandals, leaving her wondering why anyone would attack something her family and their neighbors did as a holiday present for strangers.

Maybe it was when one too many customers treated her badly on the sales floor, stressed out by the season, and disappointed not to find what they were looking for.

Or perhaps it was because her first serious relationship had fallen apart just in time for the holidays. When she was twenty-six and had been promoted to buyer, she'd gotten involved with the manager of a sister store in a large regional mall outside Portland. He was a bit older than she was and had surprised her with his interest. After only a few months, she had hopes that the relationship would turn into something serious in the New Year.

Then she discovered: (1) The man she thought was the love of her life had backstabbed her, blaming her selection of stock for his failure to reach his sales goals; (2) she was just the latest in a long line of buyers he'd romanced to get what he wanted for his store; and (3) he never, ever, kept a relationship going over the holidays, so he could be free to roam various boozy Christmas parties and take advantage of the ubiquitous mistletoe. He became, to her and to her friends, like Voldemort, he-whose-name-was-forbidden-to-be-spoken. She had vowed never again to get involved with a coworker. Running into the dipshit every few weeks had made recovering from the relationship difficult. It was only after he moved out of state that she could breathe easier during company-wide events.

Whatever the reason—a relationship gone bad, the dissatisfied customers, the ruined Christmas display—by the time she was promoted to store manager, she was fed up with Christmas, and not about to have her opinion challenged by anyone.

Between sips of wine, Hannah continued to vent to her housemate. "In addition to dealing with teacup poodles and philandering husbands, I got two new assignments today. Angie's pregnancy isn't going well, and she'll have to go on medical leave for the next few months until the baby arrives. So, on top of worrying about her and not having any luck filling the two weekend staff slots we have, now I have to organize the Christmas party Angie always worked on, too."

She sighed. "*And* Mr. Austin has decided to involve the entire chain in a huge Christmas deal for some charity. He's called a staff meeting for tomorrow before the store opens and I'll find out then what our store will be responsible for."

"Sorry to hear about Angie. I hope it works out okay. But I'm sure you can handle the extra work." Sarah raised her wineglass, but before she took another sip said, "You know, you could always convert. Being Jewish this time of year is kinda fun. I get to enjoy all the lights and songs without worrying about anything except eating too many latkes and gaining a couple pounds."

"What are you talking about? You have to buy presents for eight nights of celebrating."

"That's only if you have kids. The adults just have eight nights of good food and candle lighting. At least in my family that's how we do it."

Hannah cocked her head, a small smile appearing for the first time since she'd come home from work. "It has its appeal, believe me. Although changing religions wouldn't get me out from under the responsibility of planning the store's Christmas party. And it wouldn't make the crabby customers go away." She finished her glass of wine. "But thanks for listening. I feel better. Let me help you get dinner on the table."

"Nope. My night to cook and serve. Yours to clean up. Pour us each another glass of wine while I dish up. I made your favorite lasagna."

"The longer I live with you, the more I wonder why I'd ever want to consider marrying some guy who can't cook, doesn't pick up after himself, and never learned to do the laundry."

Sarah looked back over her shoulder with a smirk on her face. "You have to admit there are some services I don't provide that make up for the rest." She ducked when Hannah threw a pillow at her.

"I'm willing to settle for cooking these days. It's been so long since I've enjoyed any of the kind of 'services' you're talking about I've forgotten why I enjoyed them in the first place."

"Ask Santa. I hear he delivers for good girls. Although maybe that's just a rumor to make little Jewish girls jealous." Sarah was yelling from the kitchen by this time, well out of range of Hannah's pillow-throwing skills.

"Right. Santa bringing me a hot guy. With my luck I'd end up with one of his elves. Or a reindeer."

• • •

David Shay loved everything about the holiday season—the candles, the music, the decorations, even the crowds out on the rainy streets of Portland. He loved that he got to celebrate two winter holidays—he was Jewish and his family made a big deal out of Hanukkah. But his non-Jewish grandmother always made sure he enjoyed the Christmas season, too.

When he was a kid and people asked him what he wanted from Santa, David always said he was Jewish and Santa didn't come to his house. But before anyone could be embarrassed or feel sorry for him, he added, "Santa leaves my presents at Gramma's house," as if every Jewish kid had a non-Jewish relative who provided a place for Santa to leave his largesse.

As the head of the largest children's nonprofit program in Portland, David was happy to share his love for the season with the kids in the program. Usually it was a struggle to raise enough money so every one of the kids they served got something they needed, something they wanted, and something to read—the gift-giving mantra his grandmother had instilled in him. But not this year. The biggest independent bookstore in the city was donating books, and Simon Austin, owner of the only remaining locally owned retail operation, was underwriting the rest of the program.

Austin had promised David he and the employees of his eight women's stores would take care of the other two categories. Austin himself would make up the difference between what his employees collected and donated and what the program needed. In addition, there would be a generous cash donation by year's end to put the program's building campaign over the top. *And* Austin had volunteered to sponsor a holiday party for the program, at his expense and organized by the staff of his flagship store.

Simon Austin had visited the offices of SafePlace For Children and Parents the previous summer as part of a City Club of Portland committee studying the needs of children and young families in the city. David and Austin had hit it off immediately, and Austin's interest in David's program—which provided a range of services, from day care and medical help for low-income families to counseling and shelter for abused women and children—only grew with his work on the committee.

Thanks to Austin's interest, it was going to be a great holiday for SafePlace. That meant it would be a great holiday for David, who cared deeply about the program. Not just because it was his job to care, but also because the clients mattered to him. He poured his heart and soul into his work every day. Apparently that passion had convinced Simon Austin to care about SafePlace, too.

With two social workers as parents, it was unsurprising that David had ended up running a social services program. Growing up, he'd resisted the idea for a while—he couldn't see himself as an academic like his mother or a therapist like his father. But then he discovered an interest in nonprofit management. A degree in the subject and an internship with a program for victims of domestic abuse led him to SafePlace. After taking his first job there, he knew what he was meant to do with his life.

And now he was about to end a year of exciting growth and new opportunities with a bang. There would not only be enough money to make sure no kid was forgotten, but also a contribution for the building expansion, and a party to look forward to. What more could a guy want?

Well, maybe someone to share the season with. But even if David's grandmother hadn't been gone for the better part of a decade, he was pretty sure not even she could make that happen.

Chapter 2

"What do you mean, that's not enough food for two hundred people? I only have fifty employees. Even if everyone shows up and brings a date, that's still only one hundred people, max. Where did the other hundred come from?" Hannah was trying to get a few of the party details ironed out before she dug into the spreadsheets for the monthly report she was trying to get off her desk by day's end.

"And why are you worried about food for kids? You must have misunderstood. This is a party for adults. We don't include—"

"Look, I don't know what you think I was hired to do, but Angie said I needed to prepare menus for her to look at for a party of two hundred, maybe two hundred fifty people," the man at the other end of the phone call said. "And she was very clear about the need to make sure the food was kid-friendly. Not to mention allergy-free, healthful, and with a few gluten-free platters. Are you saying there's been some change in the plans?"

Hannah was too stunned to respond.

"Hey, are you still with me?" the man asked.

She shook herself out of her silence and said, "Yeah, I'm still here. I guess I need to talk to corporate and get this straightened out. I'll get back to you as soon as I do."

Without waiting for a response, she hung up the phone and yelled, "Mandy, what the hell is going on here?"

Mandy Miller, her administrative assistant, stuck her head around the edge of the doorframe. "You bellowed, my liege?"

"I just talked to the caterer Angie's been working with, and the guy said we were arranging a party for two hundred people. What's he talking about?"

"Didn't Angie tell you about the event before she left?"

"What Angie told me, between violent retching and running for the ladies' room, was I should contact Ted Reese, who turns out to be a caterer, to get the details. When I called Mr. Reese, he told me we were doing some event for two hundred or more people, including a bunch of kids." She ran her fingers through her hair hard, pulling out a few strands in frustration. "I repeat, what is he talking about?"

"Well, you'll hear the details at the meeting in an hour, but Mr. Austin has adopted a local nonprofit agency for kids as the company's Christmas charity."

"We always adopt a nonprofit at Christmas. What does that have to do with the company party?"

"I don't know that we're having the usual company Christmas party. After Mr. Austin talked to Angie a while back, she started working on a party for the charity. That's what the caterer was probably talking about. I assumed she told you. Guess you need to talk to him." Mandy looked at the clock on Hannah's desk. "Which you can do in about five minutes because he'll be here to check in with you before the meeting."

"And when did that little change of plans happen?"

"While you were on the phone. Check your email and text messages."

Hannah clicked on the icon on her computer and saw the message she'd ignored when she was talking to the caterer. "Crap. Just what I didn't need this morning."

"I hope you don't mean me," an older male voice said. A white-haired man in a dark business suit was standing in the door of her office.

Hannah stood so quickly she almost lost her balance. "Mr. Austin. No, of course I didn't mean you. I was just—" She couldn't come up with anything to finish the sentence, so she let it drift off. Gesturing to a chair, she said, "Please, come in. Have a seat."

When he moved to take it, she saw her boss wasn't alone. A younger man followed him into the office—a younger, quite deliciously good-looking man. He was a good four or five inches taller than Hannah's five foot five, with shoulders Michael Phelps would envy, big blue eyes, a scrumptious scruff of beard, and a mouth that looked like it was made to be kissed.

Which was so not what she should be thinking about. If he was there with Mr. Austin, he was work-related and off-limits. An image of the dipshit from her past flashed through her mind, and she squared her shoulders, hoping to project nothing but professional interest.

Her boss waved in the man's general direction. "Hannah, this is David Shay. He's the director of a very special program we'll be helping out this Christmas season."

The man—David, that is, he of the great body and slightly shaggy brown hair that curled around his ears and neck so adorably—joined Austin on the opposite side of Hannah's desk as the introduction continued. "David, this is Hannah Jenkins. She's the manager of this store and one of the best in my whole chain. She's on top of everything that goes on here, and probably everyplace else in the free world. I live in fear she'll decide one of these days she wants my job. She's taken over every position she's set her mind to in the decade or so she's been with us."

Hannah took the hand David Shay extended to her and used the introduction as an opportunity to look him over more intensely. The body she had already noticed filled a pair of jeans about as well as any man she'd ever seen. With them he wore a white shirt, a gold sweater, and a tan jacket. In spite of wearing no tie and what looked like hiking boots, somehow he made it all look very businesslike, even when compared to Simon Austin's bespoke tailored suit and expensive-looking tie.

"Hi, nice to meet you," David said, a smile making his already attractive face positively irresistible. His hand was warm and solid, and he held onto her just a fraction of a minute longer than necessary.

Hannah didn't say anything for a heartbeat or three, maybe four. "Um, yeah, nice to meet you," she finally got out. She had to get herself under control. Maybe if she moved away from him. She started for her small conference table to bring another chair over for him, but he seemed to read her mind and got there first.

"Is it okay if I bring this over?" he asked.

"Absolutely. Make yourself comfortable." *Well, that didn't work. Coffee. Maybe coffee would help.* She picked up the phone to summon her assistant, but she, too, seemed to be a mind reader and appeared in the doorway.

"Can I get anyone coffee? A soft drink? Sparkling water? I have your favorite, San Pellegrino, Mr. Austin," Mandy said.

"Of course you do. Hannah always makes sure you do," Austin said. "See what I mean, David? She has it all covered, down to the last detail."

David looked quite seriously at Hannah before saying, "I can believe just from looking at her that she's good at whatever she does—in the office or outside it."

• • •

David Shay was not inexperienced with beautiful women, in either business or social relationships. Usually he noted how attractive the woman looked and moved on. But Hannah Jenkins had stunned him into blurting out what was probably an inappropriate comment about the employee of the man he wanted to keep on his good side.

He hoped Mr. Austin hadn't noticed, although he wouldn't have minded if Hannah had. The way she'd looked him up and down when they shook hands had surprised him. She liked what she saw when she looked at him—that was obvious. Not that he objected. He was quite happy she might be interested.

Because he was certainly interested. The woman was seriously hot. She wasn't like the usual tall, willowy blondes he had been going out with since college. In fact, she wasn't tall at all—maybe five foot four—but she carried herself with a commanding presence that added at least a couple of inches to her actual height. Her not-blonde hair, pushed back from her face and tucked behind her ears, was some sort of reddish-brown color that looked like it might glow in the sunlight. As she turned her head, the silky mass of curly hair shifted across her shoulder. A few strands escaped confinement. He fought the urge to rub them between his fingers and inhale her clean, vanilla scent.

Green eyes that looked intelligent, a body that looked killer, even in the very serious black suit she wore with a white shirt, and the endorsement of the smartest businessman David had ever met presented a picture of a woman who intrigued him and who he'd like to know better. Much, much better.

And with that handshake they'd shared, he was sure she felt the connection he did. He'd expected to see sparks emanate from their hands when they touched, and was almost disappointed when it hadn't happened.

"I brought David in to meet you today, Hannah, because I expect you'll be seeing a lot of him around here over the next few weeks. His program, SafePlace for Children and Parents, is this year's charity for the company. There'll be the usual gifts and donations, but this year, I've decided to make a change in the Christmas party we always have. Attendance has been falling off at our annual Christmas Eve staff get-together. On top of that, a number of people have said it would be nice to see where their donations went. So this year, we'll be delivering the gifts to David's kids in person at a party we'll be hosting at his facility. Angie's already started on it." He turned to David. "Angie Colleto is the assistant manager here, David." He smiled at Hannah. "I hope you don't mind I went over your head and talked to her about it last month."

"I don't mind, of course, but I'm afraid Angie's out of the loop, Mr. Austin. As of yesterday, she's home on medical leave. Her obstetrician wants her in bed for the next few months."

"I'm sorry to hear that. Is it serious?"

"Well, not so serious that she's in the hospital, but serious enough that she'll be out for the duration of her pregnancy."

"You'll let me know if there's anything the company can do for her, won't you? I don't want her to lack for good care."

"Thank you, Mr. Austin. I'll let her know. I'm sure she'll appreciate it."

"But that means we need someone else to work with David on this project."

"She left me with a contact for the caterer, and I talked to him this morning." Hannah shrugged, as if it was nothing, but looked as if she was fighting a frown.

Simon Austin must have picked up the same vibe. "Does that add too much to what you already have to do for the holidays? I don't want you to feel like you've been asked to take on more than you're comfortable doing."

"It's all good, Mr. Austin. Don't worry about it. I can manage, even if it's not the store's usual Christmas party."

"No, it's a party for all my people, plus all of yours," David said. "I apologize for making your job harder. Whatever I can do to help, I'll do. It must be a circus, working retail during the holidays."

"Circus. Zoo. Mosh pit. War zone. Take your pick. It's any of those things on any given day."

"But you love it, don't you, Hannah?" Austin said. "We all do. Christmas is such a happy time of year. Everyone is in a giving mood."

David thought she seemed reluctant to say what she really felt. *Interesting*, he thought. *She's obviously one of Simon's best employees, but she's trying to hide something. Not letting him see something she's sure he won't like. Is it about his store? Or something else?*

"I'm always happy to see the sales figures from this time of year, Mr. Austin, that's for sure. It's the best thing about the season."

"Well, this year, the best thing will be what we're able to do for David's program. I'll let him tell you what he needs and what I've agreed to provide for him, then I'll answer any questions you have. I want to make sure we're on the same page before we go into the meeting today to announce the program to the rest of your staff."

• • •

Hannah listened, trying to take in what David Shay was saying. It wasn't easy. Part of her brain screamed in protest at having to plan an event for two hundred people when she already had plenty of other things to handle. Another part of her—perhaps not so much her mind—drooled over the man she would get to work with on a close and personal basis.

As he went on describing his program, her protesting brain pointed out that, no matter how hot he was, he was a work colleague. He was not a candidate for any attention she or her hormones wanted to give him. Besides, she was already up to her ears in alligators—or teacup poodles, depending on the day—all without her assistant manager and down two sales associates. There was no time for the distraction of wayward hormones.

Crap. David had stopped talking. He and Mr. Austin were looking at her as if they expected her to say something. She had no idea what they wanted. "Sorry, I got sidetracked while you were talking. It was rude of me. Can you repeat what you said?"

David smiled. "All of it, or just the part where I asked how you wanted to handle the kids' Santa letters?"

"Just that part will be fine. I heard the rest, but was so busy thinking of ways to set up the giving tree my mind wandered." She hoped the little white lie would pass without comment, but the look on David's face pretty much told her he knew what she was really thinking about. "Do the kids write out the letters by hand?"

"Yes, or the moms do for the littler ones."

"If you could get me the originals, I'd like that. I was thinking maybe I'd put the letter—or a copy of it—in an envelope on the giving tree. Put the name, age, and sex of the child on the envelope and let people pick who they want." She turned to David again. "Are the letters simply a list?"

"Sometimes. But often there's something else, maybe a bit about the child writing it. Sometimes a request for something for a sibling or a parent instead of for themselves. It varies."

"That's what I was hoping. The more information there is, the more my staff will feel connected. It'll spark their interest, get them involved."

"Sounds great. I'll deliver the letters to you as soon as I get them," David said.

Mr. Austin grinned and smacked the desk twice with the flat of his hand. "I told you we'd get behind this, David. I was counting on Angie, but it's even better with Hannah in charge. She's got her finger on the pulse of the holiday season. It'll be a great event." He rose from the chair. "On to the staff meeting. Let's get it over with so we can all get back to work." Without waiting for a response, he headed for the door. David Shay followed.

"I'll be along in two minutes, Mr. Austin. I have one more thing to do here," Hannah said.

Which was, as soon as her office door closed, to put her head down on the desk and moan. It was a *Tale of Two Cities* moment—the best of times, the worst of times. She would be working with the cutest guy she'd met in years, which put him on the no-date list, *and* this project was just one more thing she would have to fake her way through in the holiday season she had come to dislike.

Fate had one hell of a sense of humor.

• • •

After Mr. Austin opened the meeting and David had given a brief description of his program, Hannah took over. David admired the professional and enthusiastic way she handled her part. By the time she'd outlined her ideas for the giving tree and what they might do for the party, she had a forest of hands raised, eager to help. She motivated her staff as naturally and easily as most people ordered coffee.

Nevertheless, when she wasn't "on," when she wasn't doing her part of the presentation, David thought he could see an expression on her face that looked somewhat less than enthusiastic about the assignment she'd just been handed. He decided it might be a good idea to see what was going on. At least, that was the reason he gave himself for hanging back to talk with her.

He turned down Mr. Austin's offer of coffee, and instead loitered around the meeting room, staring intently at his phone as if reading his emails and messages—although he wasn't doing either. Finally Austin left, and Hannah finished a conversation with one of her staff. As soon as she made for the door, he followed her.

"Hannah, wait up for a minute, will you?" he called. He was relieved to see her stop immediately.

"Is there something else I can do for you, David?" she asked, her eyes glued to her phone, which he was sure, unlike his own, was actually turned on.

"Yes, you can grab a cup of coffee with me. I want to ask you something."

She looked up, then consulted her phone again. "I don't have a lot of time today. Can you just ask it now?"

"Okay. If that's what you'd rather." He rubbed the back of his neck and shook his head. "I'm not sure how to say this without offending you, but I get the feeling your heart's not really in the idea of working with my program. Am I wrong?"

She laughed. "Yes, you're wrong. I'm impressed with what I just heard and happy we can do something to help."

"Then what was with the look on your face when Simon talked about 'helping out in the holiday spirit'? You looked like it was the last thing on earth you wanted to do."

He thought he saw a flash of surprise cross her face, but it was gone so quickly he was almost convinced he'd imagined it.

"No, it's nothing like that." She turned to go.

He put his hand on her forearm to detain her. The warmth of her skin seeping through the sleeve of her jacket almost sidetracked him. "Wait. Please. I didn't imagine the look on your face when Simon was talking. If it's not that you don't want to work with my program, what is it?"

She stared at the ground for a moment. When she turned to face him, she wore the same professional expression on her face he'd seen when he and Simon Austin had first invaded her office.

"It's nothing that will keep me from doing a great job on the party or the giving tree. Your kids and their parents will have a perfect holiday. Don't worry."

"I'm not worried about them. I'm wondering about you."

She closed her eyes and sighed. "You don't give up, do you?"

"Nope. It's my most annoying habit. So you might as well just answer the question."

She seemed to be biting back a smile. "Well, at least if I'm going to work with you, I now know your worst habit."

"I didn't say it was my worst habit. I said it was my most annoying one. And you still haven't told me what I want to know."

The smile broke through for a few moments before the serious look returned. "Okay. If you must know, I don't like Christmas. And listening to all that talk of how happy everyone is during the season turned me off."

"Really? What's not to like about an excuse to get presents and eat cookies?"

She didn't laugh at his attempt to lighten the conversation. "Cookies and presents are great. But the season also brings out the worst in people. They're nasty and unpleasant to deal with. They're rude. They yell. They act like barbarians. No one seems happy, no matter how many gifts and goodies they have. If I could go to sleep after Thanksgiving dinner and wake up on New Year's Day, I'd be a happy camper."

"Wow. That must make it hard to do what you do for a living. Although you seem good at covering it up. You could have fooled me with that speech you gave in there."

"That had nothing to do with Christmas. That had everything to do with making this work for your kids. It's important for them. And that's important to Mr. Austin. I'm not about to let him—or you—down."

"So, when you're not trying to please your boss, you're, what, like Scrooge? I don't remember him being quite as beautiful as you are."

The color rising on her cheeks was the only indication she'd registered his compliment. "I'm afraid I'm very close to sharing Ebenezer's original opinion of the holidays, although I don't believe I've ever uttered the words 'bah, humbug' until just this moment. Now if you'll excuse me, I have a to-do list that won't quit and need to get back to my office. Just let me know when you have those Santa letters, will you please?"

"I will. And let me know what I can do to make this easier on you. I'm willing to help with whatever you need."

She nodded, her attention back on her smartphone.

David watched her walk away and smiled. There was nothing he liked more than a challenge. And, whether she knew it or not, Ms. Hannah Jenkins had just handed him one. All he had to do was figure out how to deal with it.

Chapter 3

"Mandy, isn't it? I don't know if you remember me. I was here a week ago with Mr. Austin. I'm David Shay, the—"

"Of course I remember you. I never forget a cute guy." Mandy winked at him. "What can I do for you?"

David had been afraid Mandy would be overprotective of her boss. But now it sounded like it might be easier than he thought to pump her for information. "First, you can tell me if Hannah's around and also if she has plans for lunch."

"That's first and second, isn't it? But never mind. Yes, she's here. She's holed up in her office working on some report or other. And there's nothing on her calendar. You want me to pencil you in and pretend the appointment's been there for days and she's forgotten?"

David laughed. "That sounds like something my assistant would do. I can see I should never let the two of you get together and plot."

"Too late. We've already been talking about the party. And who knows where that will lead."

"How long have you worked for Hannah?"

"She inherited me when she was promoted. I've been the administrative assistant to every manager in this store for twenty years."

"Twenty years? Did you start working when you were in kindergarten?"

"Don't you know better than to flirt with women old enough to be your mother? It's a strain on our old hearts."

David glanced around the office as if hoping for reinforcements. "This is a tough room to play, isn't it?"

"If you think this is a tough room, wait until you get in there." Mandy motioned toward the closed door to what David knew was Hannah's office.

"Are you trying to scare me off?"

"No, just warning you what might happen." Mandy paused for a moment, as if thinking about how to say something. "Look, I shouldn't, but I'll let you in on a little secret. Hannah's not as tough as she pretends to be. If you're patient, she'll eventually show you how to find the door in the wall she's built up around her."

"I'm grateful for the heads-up, but curious why you're willing to tell me this."

"Mr. Austin thinks the world of you. And I've never known him to be wrong in his assessment of a person. If he trusts you that much, you might be the man who can get past the façade Hannah's put up ever since ... " She shook off the end of the sentence. "Anyway, I thought from the sparks I saw between the two of you last week, I might give you a little help. I'm more than her guardian at the gate. I'm her friend, too."

David was definitely curious about what Mandy wasn't telling him, but smart enough not to push. "From what I can see, you do both things well. So, I'll impose for one more question—would you tell me what her favorite lunch restaurant is?"

"She hardly ever leaves the building for lunch, but on the rare occasions she does, she likes Thai food."

"Nice to know. Thanks." He started toward the closed door. "I know a good Thai restaurant not far from here."

"Good luck getting her to go with you." Mandy bolted from her chair and headed him off. "Wait. Let me announce you."

"She doesn't like surprise visitors?"

A huge grin broke out on Mandy's face. "No, she's fine with surprises. I want to see her face when she sees you're here."

• • •

Hannah was up to her ears in a sales report when Mandy knocked on her office door and peeked in to say, "My lady, you have a visitor."

"Oh, crap. Did I get so wound up in this stuff I forgot about an appointment?"

"No, you don't have an appointment. You have ... "

"An unexpected guest," David Shay said as he came into the office.

Mandy had a goofy grin on her face as she popped back to her side of the door and closed it.

"I hope I'm not interrupting anything," David said.

Hannah resisted the temptation to make sure her hair was neat and her shirt unwrinkled. "No, you're not. To what do I owe this ... ?" She stopped, not wanting to reveal that it was a pleasure to see him standing at her office door. "This ... visit," she finished.

David perched on the edge of her desk not two feet away from her, the smile he aimed at her seeming to indicate he knew how the sentence was originally supposed to end. "Well, the ostensible reason was to bring you the Santa letters you asked for last week. But hidden behind that was the hope I could talk you into having lunch with me. And, since you can see from my empty hands that I forgot the letters, I'm forced to confess upfront my real reason for being here, not the one I was faking." He put out his hands, palms up, as if to show her how empty they were.

"So, if you are really the amazing woman Simon Austin thinks you are, you'll take pity on me, overlook my intention of using the Christmas hopes of innocent children as an excuse to ask you to lunch, and just say yes, even though I failed to bring you what you asked for."

As hard as she tried, Hannah couldn't help laughing. "That was the most pathetic invitation to lunch I've ever heard."

"It was, wasn't it?"

"You say that so proudly."

"I'm proud that I got you to laugh. Did it get me lunch with you?"

Hannah wasn't sure if he was flirting or merely making nice because Mr. Austin was being so generous to SafePlace. And she was even less sure whether spending any time with him was a good idea. Although he was as tempting as a pan of brownies just out of the oven—sweet, dark, hot.

Stop. Just stop. However attractive he was, she had to work with him. Which meant it broke her no-personal-contact-with-colleagues rule to consider him as anything but a business associate. But she couldn't be rude, either.

"I really don't have time for lunch in a restaurant someplace" she said. "But maybe we could grab a quick sandwich and swing by your office so I can get those letters. I need to see your common area where we'll be having the party anyway. Your building isn't far from here, is it?"

David hopped off the desk and extended his hand to her to help her out of her chair. "Nope. And there's a food truck parked nearby that makes great gyros."

She pointedly ignored the proffered hand. "One of my favorite sandwiches. Let's go." Preceding him out of her office, she waved at her assistant as she walked past. "I'll be back in an hour, Mandy. And I have my phone if you need me." She swore she saw David give Mandy a thumbs-up.

• • •

A short walk, a bit of a wait in line at the food truck, and they had their gyros. David led her to his office, where he cleared off one end of his desk.

"I thought we'd eat in here instead of out in the common room. It's often crowded and noisy at lunch. Sometimes lunch at my desk isn't a punishment, it's a pleasure. No one interrupts."

As if to prove him wrong, a woman walked into the office. "David," she said, "I need to talk to you about ... " She seemed to suddenly realize he wasn't alone. "Oops. Sorry. I didn't know you had someone in here. I'll come back later."

"Thanks, Jenny. I'll be here all afternoon."

But Jenny was just the first of a spate of staff and clients, who needed—or wanted—to see him. He was patient with every one of them, never short-tempered or abrupt. He put off his staff until later in the afternoon, but he answered the questions of the two program clients who had been part of the parade of people.

After handling his fifth request, he apologized. "I'm sorry about this. There've been so many interruptions we haven't had much of a chance to talk about the party. I don't know where it all came from today."

"It's okay. I got to eat an amazing gyro. They really are good, if a little messy."

"There's a staff bathroom to the right and down the hall. You can wash up there while I clean up the desk."

When she got to the bathroom and saw the mess the gyros had made of her face, Hannah wasn't sure merely washing up would be enough. Tahini sauce had dribbled out of her mouth onto her chin and dripped over her hands and down her arms. A shower might have been more effective.

A shower. The image of being in a shower with David flashed through her mind and had to be banished before it took up residence there. What was wrong with her? She'd never fantasized about a man she barely knew. Okay, maybe some movie star, but not a guy in real life. She took a few moments to get her thoughts under control before returning to his office.

David's smile when he saw her almost resurrected her shower fantasy. Only this time she needed a cold shower to cool off from the heat his smile generated in her. She shifted focus from his mouth to the bulging manila envelope he handed her.

"The Santa letters you want. There are a few more kids who should be getting their letters to me by week's end."

"Thanks. I'll get our IT guy on this."

"IT? I thought you were doing the giving tree."

"I'll put up an actual giving tree in the staff break room at my store, but I thought it would be a good idea for people in the other stores in the chain to participate, too, so we're setting up a virtual giving tree. One of the IT staff volunteered to create and maintain it. He was excited to be able to help. I'll send you the link when it goes live."

David handed her a business card. "My email address is on there. So's my cell number. You know, in case you have a Christmas party emergency after business hours and need my help." He cocked his head and gave her a winsome smile. Again. "Actually, I'd be glad to help even if it's not an emergency."

"I don't plan on having Christmas party emergencies during or after business hours. I've got it all under control, but thanks." Letting him help would take some of the responsibility off her. And she'd get to spend time with him.

But those were also the reasons to turn him down. No way would she let anyone, especially someone who could relay the information to Mr. Austin, think she couldn't handle her assignments. And more time with him meant more temptation. She didn't need that.

She started for the door. "I should get back to my office, but before I go, can I take a look at your common area and kitchen? I promised the committee in charge of food and decorations I'd give them some idea of what they have to work with."

David led her to a large, light, and airy open space with tables and chairs scattered around and colorful bulletin boards decorated with children's work on all the walls. Three of the larger boards already had a few holiday decorations on them.

"Wow. Decorations up and it's barely December. You're really into the holidays, aren't you?" Hannah said.

"I love the winter holidays. And we have kids who celebrate just about everything—Christmas, Kwanzaa, Hanukkah, Winter Solstice, even Ramadan if it falls late in the year. I try to recognize all the traditions, even if they're not mine."

She hesitated for a moment. "I saw a menorah in your office. Is that your tradition?"

"Yup, I'm Jewish. The staff and whoever's around light candles every night of Hanukkah before we leave work."

"Interesting. You're Jewish, but you love Christmas?"

"And everything else people celebrate this time of the year. I had a non-Jewish grandmother who instilled the love for Christmas in me, as well as parents who loved Hanukkah. It was easy to extend that affection to anything else that happens in winter."

"No wonder you don't understand us Scrooge-like people. You're like Tiny Tim or something."

"A bit older. Considerably less physically challenged, but the attitude's pretty close."

Hannah sighed. "I wish I could share your enthusiasm. It would make life a lot easier in December. Maybe I need to have a couple ghosts visit me."

David tapped his forefinger on his mouth. "Hmm. There's an idea. I'm no ghost, but I have a suggestion." He put out his hand, palm up. "Make a bet with me."

"A bet. About what?"

"I bet that by the time our Christmas party is over, I can convince you not only to like Christmas, but even to believe that Santa Claus, at least in spirit, exists."

Hannah snorted. "I don't make bets I know I'll win."

"I can be very persuasive."

She pushed his hand away. "Nobody's that good. Not even you."

"Humor me. We'll play by Dickens's rules—he had three ghosts convince Scrooge. Give me three tries to show you how much fun this time of year can be."

She was headed down the slipperiest of slopes spending time with him. She knew that. The only safe answer was "no way." Why was it so hard to say those two simple words? It's not like she really wanted to learn to like Christmas anyway. But instead of "no," what came out of her mouth was, "What's in if for me when I win?"

"I'll stand in front of the Christmas tree in Pioneer Courthouse Square and denounce the entire season and all its manifestations."

Hannah giggled. "And you have to write a Scroogey editorial for the paper."

"Okay. But what do I get when I win?"

"Believe me, you won't. But I guess I should indulge you. What would you like to win?"

He wiggled his eyebrows up and down and shot an exaggerated leer at her. "I can think of a number of things I'd like to win from you, but how about this—*when* I win, I get a kiss from you on New Year's Eve."

Oh, crap. Now what had she gotten herself into? Kissing him? On New Year's? Why couldn't she just walk away?

"A kiss. On New Year's Eve."

"Yup."

"What will your date, whoever she is, say about that?"

"I doubt very much that will be a problem."

She was afraid to ask why. No, that wasn't right. She was afraid she already knew why. But it wouldn't matter. No one, not even David Shay, could convince her to like the holidays. He didn't have a chance of winning this bet. She'd be home alone on New Year's Eve, just like she'd been last year and the year before and the year before that.

It was a sure thing. She couldn't lose. "Okay, you're on."

• • •

On the walk back to her office, Hannah tried to figure out why she'd agreed to the bet with David. It wasn't about winning. She knew she was going to win. That wasn't in question. But it was out of character for her to agree to spend time with him on what he didn't call dates but which she suspected he meant as just that. So what had made her say yes to this man who was a virtual stranger? One who was, admittedly, massively attractive. But other than that, what did she really know about him, anyway? She knew he had such a large dose of confidence that he felt free to challenge her core belief in the foolishness of Christmas. And he cared enough about the holidays that he'd caused her to cross a line in the sand she'd drawn about dating people she worked with. She also knew he'd impressed Mr. Austin, which, she had to admit, said something good about him.

But that was the sum of what she knew about David Shay.

However, if he meant what he said, she would soon get to know him a lot better. Her imagination—and those pesky hormones—ran wild at what that could mean. She had to put a stop to that line of thinking. This would be nothing more than meeting with a colleague. Just meetings. With an attractive, sexy colleague who had shown up in a number of her recent fantasies.

Oh, crap. That wasn't working. She'd have to work on a better line of defense.

When she walked back into her office, Mandy looked up from her computer and grinned.

"So, it looks like you had a good lunch."

"If you like gyros, I know where to find good ones. A food truck near the SafePlace building."

"I have a feeling it was more than gyros that put that smile on your face."

Hannah dumped the envelope full of Santa letters on Mandy's desk. "For that, you get to work on the giving tree project. I need all these letters copied and sorted by sex and age. I want to take them home with me tonight to work on."

"Your wish is my command, my liege." Mandy stood up and threw a crisp salute at her boss.

Hannah shook her head and tried not to smile. "You can skip the fake obedience. Just get the damn letters copied."

"How about 'as you wish'? Does that sound better?" Mandy asked.

Hannah kept her response to herself. Her assistant would love to know that she thought it would sound better in certain intimate settings in the baritone voice of one David Shay.

Chapter 4

It took David a while to figure out a plan to convince Hannah to enjoy the holidays. When he finally did, he called her. She was in a meeting. And when she called back, he'd turned his phone off so he could give his full attention to a new client. After a couple more rounds of telephone tag, he sent her a text asking her to meet him in his office after work the following Friday. There was something he wanted to show her, and then they could grab a bite to eat.

Stage one of "The Plan" was to lure her into getting involved with the kids who would be there that day to set up the Christmas tree and the displays for Kwanzaa and Hanukkah. How could anyone resist the kids' excitement? If anything could begin to soften her up about the holiday, that should do it.

• • •

Hannah was a bit early arriving at SafePlace for what she was still calling just a meeting, not a date. She found David in the common area. He was busy unpacking boxes of Christmas ornaments; kente cloth, candleholders, and fabric art fruits for the Kwanzaa display; and dreidels, gelt, and menorahs for Hanukkah. When he didn't notice her right away, she stayed close to the door, watching him at a task he obviously enjoyed as he chatted with the kids and his staff who were helping. Eventually he looked over and saw her. He grinned as he strode across the room.

"I'm sorry. I was so wrapped up in getting things out for the kids I wasn't paying attention."

She smiled. "Don't apologize. I'm early, and you were obviously having fun."

"This is one of our favorite days this time of year. The kids can't wait to get here after school to get the tree set up and the Kwanzaa and Hanukkah displays organized."

"No Ramadan display?" she said with a grin. "No winter solstice?"

"Ramadan was early this year. We've already done our display about that. And eventually one of the bulletin boards will have a display explaining the movement of celestial bodies and how that makes the seasons change. We've found that to be more acceptable to a lot of parents than an explanation of Wiccan solstice rituals." He tugged at her hand. "Come meet some of the staff. And you're welcome to help, if you'd like. If it's okay with you, I'd like to finish up here before we go to dinner."

"Thanks, but I'll watch. I'm not much of a decorator."

"Neither am I. Actually, I'm only useful because I can reach higher on the tree than the kids can. But I get such a kick out of it I can't stay away."

After being introduced to his staff, she found a seat at one of the only tables not directly involved in the decorating. At first, what was going on looked like chaos. There must have been two or three dozen kids, maybe more—it was hard to count them when they were moving around so much—unpacking boxes, hanging ornaments, setting up displays, and pinning things on the bulletin boards. But after watching for a few minutes, she realized that although the kids seemed to have free rein to set things up the way they wanted them, every activity had adults overseeing it. David and two others were working on the Christmas tree, two staff members were setting up the Kwanzaa table, and two more were at the Hanukkah table. And as each of the displays was set up, the adults in charge kept up a running commentary on the origins and meaning of the different holiday items.

In what seemed like no time at all, the chaos resulted in two table displays and one tree completely decorated with great care and attention—if not with designer style. Hannah had to admit it was fun to watch.

David seemed to give a few last-minute suggestions to his staff before coming over to her again. "I'm about finished. Five more minutes and ... "

A little girl with a blonde ponytail interrupted by tugging at his hand. "David," she said, "I finished my Santa letter." She handed him a folded piece of paper. "But I'm worried."

He knelt down so he was on her level. "What are you worried about, kiddo?"

"How's Santa going to know where I am? Maybe he won't be able to find me because we had to move."

"Santa always knows where kids are. It's one of the things he does best."

She obviously wasn't convinced. "Are you sure?"

"Absolutely."

She sighed. "Okay. I guess you know."

He stood up and pointed at a table in the back. "Hey, I think the cookies and milk have arrived. Why don't you grab some before they're all gone?"

The little girl smiled and ran to where the snacks were being dispensed to the kid decorators.

"What's her story?" Hannah asked. "Why is she here?"

"Let's just say her mother left a really bad situation so she and her kids could have a violence-free future."

Hannah shuddered at the idea that anyone would hurt that adorable little girl. "She's, what, five? Six?"

"Almost six, and her brother's four. We're trying to find a permanent safe place for them but probably won't be able to before the end of the year, so they'll be in the shelter 'til then."

On an impulse, Hannah walked over to where the little girl was eating her cookie and sat down in a chair next to her. "Hi, my name's Hannah, and I'm one of Santa's helpers this year. I promise you," with her forefinger she made an X across her chest, "cross my heart, that Santa will get your letter. And I'll tell him where you are so your presents won't get lost."

"Is your name really Hannah? My name's Hannah, too." The little girl's grin was so big it almost cracked her face. It definitely broke the adult Hannah's heart.

"Well then, Hannah, too, that makes it even more important I make sure Santa knows where you are. Us Hannahs have to look out for each other."

The little Hannah threw her arms around the older Hannah's neck. "Thank you so much, Hannah One."

"Hannah One?"

"If I'm Hannah, too, you're Hannah One, aren't you?"

"I guess I am." Hannah One laughed at the impish look on the little girl's face.

"When you tell him where I am, can you tell him about my brother, too?"

"Of course. What's your brother's name?"

"George."

Grown-up Hannah made a great show of taking a piece of paper and a pen out of her purse and writing down the information. "There. I have it all. Santa will be sure to get your gifts to the right place."

As she walked back across the room, she saw the soft look in David's eyes. "Don't go thinking this is making me a convert to Christmas," she said quietly when she was close enough for him to hear.

"I'd never think anything like that about a hardnosed Scrooge like you." But his smile betrayed his words. "I'll add Hannah's letter to the ones I have in the office for you, and you can—"

She grabbed the letter. "Nope. Don't get it mixed in with the others. She's mine. And I want her brother's, too."

From the expression on his face, David was thinking about saying something else to her, something gloat-y, she thought. But he didn't. He merely put his hand at the small of her back, and pointed her toward his office. "Let's go get the rest of those letters and get out of here. I'm starving. If we don't get dinner soon, I'm going to steal the cookies from the kids, and that wouldn't look good on my next performance evaluation from my board."

• • •

It couldn't have gone any better if he'd orchestrated it. David had hoped seeing the kids so excited about the holidays would open Hannah's eyes a bit to the real meaning of the season. What he hadn't foreseen was the arrival of a six-year-old heartbreaker who shared Hannah's name. This was date one, and a little blonde cutie had achieved exactly what he'd wanted for this stage of the plan. Hannah Jenkins was now invested in making Christmas merry for a couple of kids. Now he could focus at dinner on getting to know her for personal reasons, not because of the bet he'd made.

Because Mandy had told him Hannah liked Thai food, he headed for Pok Pok, the best Thai restaurant in town. After they'd ordered, they settled into a Dating 101 conversation, exchanging information about families, colleges, work experience. They branched out into books and movies they liked, music that spoke to them, discovering considerable overlap.

But the most interesting part of the conversation followed after Hannah asked if he had plans for the future other than managing SafePlace.

"I've never given much thought to doing anything else," he said. "I'm happy where I am and have plans for expanding the program. There's need in the suburbs I'd like to see about meeting. You can't imagine how many women and children are at risk outside the city." He was sure his expression wasn't exactly warm and fuzzy, thanks to the images of what he'd seen in the shelter that popped into his head.

She grasped his hand. The little jolt of attraction he felt from the contact brought him back to where he was and who he was with. He shook his head and shrugged off the mood. "Sorry. Didn't mean to sound so serious." He squeezed her hand. "What about you? What's your secret plan for the future?"

"It's going to sound shallow and vain after what you just said."

"The drive to do something you love is never shallow or vain. Tell me."

"Well, as frivolous as it sounds, I want to design clothes for young women starting their careers. The kind they can buy without a lot of money, but still look professional and smart. Actually, I already design clothes. And make them. But only for myself and my friends. Someday, maybe, I'd like to do it for a clothing company."

"Creativity isn't frivolous. And it sounds like you've found a niche worth filling. Have you tried contacting the clothing companies around here with some of your designs?"

"Columbia Sportswear and Nike aren't exactly my style."

He looked at the form-fitting rose-colored jacket she wore with black fabric roses on one shoulder. "Even I can see that. So what are you doing to find a company that *is* your style?"

She shook her head. "Nothing at the moment. I just do it for fun. Maybe one of these years I'll think about doing it for real."

The arrival of their main courses stopped the conversation about her dreams, but David tucked the information away, sure he would find it useful eventually.

• • •

As far as Hannah was concerned, the evening couldn't have been much better. Her favorite food at the city's best Thai restaurant, a hot guy across the table from her, and some of the most interest-ing conversation she'd had with anyone, male or female, in ages. David Shay was funny, smart, and obviously invested in what he did. She'd seen the hurt in his eyes when he talked about his cli-ents. And he hadn't made fun of her for wanting to design clothes. He seemed to understand how much it meant to her.

But now the question of the evening was about to arise. Would he kiss her? She realized she wanted him to—and was even willing to make the move herself she was so drawn to him. The spark of attraction he'd lit had been obvious to her from the day he walked into her office, and it hadn't cooled in the two times she'd seen him since, no matter how much she told herself not to get involved with him. And then there was the way he looked tonight when he talked about the clients his program served. Surely someone who cared so much about other people wouldn't be ... couldn't be ... a jerk like the dipshit. Would he?

He followed her directions to head south, to her house in Sellwood. After he pulled his CRV up to the curb and cut the engine, he said, "Your house is cute."

"Thanks, but it's not mine. It belongs to my housemate. I rent from her." She hesitated for a moment before saying, "I'd invite you in to meet her, but I didn't give her any warning about bringing someone home with me. And given how she dresses down when she gets home, I'd embarrass her by springing you on her unannounced."

"Maybe the next time." He unclipped his seatbelt and slid closer to her. "And there will be a next time, won't there?"

"Of course there will be. This was only your first opportunity to show me where I've erred in my thinking about Christmas. We have to get through two more before I win the bet."

"*Get through?* Is that how you look at going out with me?"

She could feel the blush rising on her face. If she was lucky, it was dark enough in the car that he couldn't see. "I didn't mean it that way. I just meant ... "

"If you meant you're still convinced I can't win but are happy to know we'll be spending time together, I'll rein in my outrage." He released her seatbelt and tugged at her to move her toward him. "I want to think you'd like to see me again, regardless of the bet." He took her face in his hands and began to stroke her cheekbones with his thumbs.

She couldn't breathe for a few seconds. The warmth of his hands, the pressure of his caress drove any response she might have made from her thoughts. Just as she began to think cogently again, he touched her mouth with his, lightly, softly. She could taste the spice from his dinner on his lips, along with a very distinctly male flavor.

He tilted her head to get her mouth exactly where he wanted it and kissed her again—this time with more intensity, his lips parting and his tongue urging her to open for him. A moan sounded, echoing inside the car. She was pretty sure it came from her.

Her arms went around his neck, and he pulled her closer, over the console between the seats. It should have been uncomfortable, but all she could feel was the heat of his mouth, the slick of his tongue as he explored her lips from one corner to the other then found her tongue and played hide-and-seek with it.

He slid one hand up her side so it was just under an aching breast. Arching her back to give him better access, she encouraged him to touch the nipple now puckered in anticipation.

But he broke from the kiss. "Not yet. Not tonight. Not in a dark car. I want more than that for us. With lots more time." He kissed her forehead, the tip of her nose and her lips. "You are the most delicious thing I've ever tasted. Do you know that?"

She giggled. "You taste like Thai food."

"Luckily for me, you like Thai food. So all I have to do is find a toothpaste and mouthwash that tastes like pad Thai, and I won't have to worry about keeping you interested."

He was funny and smart. He kissed like a wicked romance hero, and he talked about wanting to keep her interested. Any one of those characteristics would intrigue her. The combination would keep her awake for quite a while, wondering if she wanted to be interested.

Chapter 5

It had been another miserable day in the Christmas trenches. First there was the crew of teenaged shoplifters, a classic "gang that couldn't shoot straight," they were so inept at what they tried to do. Unfortunately, their parents refused to believe the evidence of the security cameras or the undercover shoppers who saw the teens stuffing merchandise into the bags they were caught with. The indulgent parents argued for what seemed like hours about how their darlings were being harassed before threatening lawsuits and letters of complaint.

Then there was the man who drove her most experienced salesperson to tears with demands for things the store couldn't provide—alterations to merchandise purchased at another shop, champagne to accompany the diamond bracelet he claimed to be about to purchase, women's sizes that didn't exist in clothing meant for young teens, not adults. Her staffer didn't call in the reinforcements until things spiraled out of control, so Hannah knew another angry letter would be winging its way to Mr. Austin soon.

And that was just what happened before lunchtime.

Worn out when she got home, Hannah changed into yoga pants and a knit top before pouring herself a largish glass of wine. It was her night to cook, but she was beyond the ability to even think about what to prepare, let alone cook it. She was rummaging for takeout menus when her cell rang.

"What're you up to tonight?" David asked, sounding altogether too cheerful for her mood.

"A tall glass of wine, some pad Thai, and bed. How about you?"

"You tempt me, but ... "

"I don't remember asking you to join me. Did I?"

"Sorry. I jumped to a conclusion based on what I wanted, not on what you said." Before she could say anything more, he continued, "Actually, what I called for might turn your day around. I have the urge to go see one of my favorite holiday places in Portland. I'd like to take you with me. Then I'll buy you an Irish coffee or a hot buttered rum."

"Thanks but I'm not really in the mood to go anyplace tonight."

"If you go with me, that'll change, I guarantee."

She apparently hesitated long enough for him to assume she was going to say "yes," because he said, "Good. I'll be there in twenty minutes. Dress warmly. We'll be outside for a while." And he hung up.

Hannah punched the number to call him back and cancel, but she ended the call before the first ring. Maybe he was right, if not for the reason he said. Some Christmas display wasn't likely to improve her frame of mind, but being with him might—especially if there was any chance for another kiss like the one that ended their last outing. He could put anyone in a good mood with his kisses.

After changing into a pair of jeans and a sweater, she dug out a down jacket and found a warm scarf, hat, and gloves. A quick note to Sarah explained why there was no dinner waiting and warned her David might come back to the house after their date. No, not date, she reminded herself. An outing. A meeting with a colleague.

Except how many meetings with colleagues ended with a kiss?

She was at the front door in time to unlock it just as he knocked.

"Eager to see me? I like that in a woman," he said, bending down to give her a peck on the cheek.

"Eager to get this over with so we can get to the hot buttered rum and dinner."

"Did I say anything about dinner?"

"No, but if you're dragging me out of my warm house to see some stupid Christmas display before I've eaten, there better be dinner involved."

"The place I have in mind for our drinks does food. But first the Christmas cheer, Ebenezer."

He drove north until they reached Hawthorne Boulevard, where he turned east. At Cesar Chavez Boulevard, he turned north again.

"Oh, my God. It's the fifteenth of December, isn't it? Are you taking me where I think you're taking me?" Hannah asked.

"How do you know where we're headed?"

"I don't know, but I think we're headed to my old neighborhood."

His head snapped toward her so fast she thought she heard his neck crack. "Are you saying you lived around here?"

"I grew up around here." Now it was her turn to be mysterious.

"Where, exactly?"

"Oh, a block or so over from here." She waved vaguely in the general direction of east. "Look, there's a parking place. You better grab it. Parking's tough around here this time of year."

"You know exactly where I'm taking you, don't you?" he said as he slipped his car into the spot she'd pointed out.

"Yup. Peacock Lane. I might have known a Christmas freak like you would love the place." She hopped out of the car and waited on the sidewalk for him.

"You know the street?"

"I *lived* on the street until I went off to college."

"How can someone who lived at ground zero for Christmas spirit be a Scrooge?" He took her hand, and they joined the crowds on foot headed for the light display on the street.

"I admit I loved the lights when I lived here. For a couple of weeks every year, it felt like we were the center of the city's attention." She looked around at the crowd. "I haven't been here in years. It looks even more popular than I remember it."

"So your parents don't live here anymore?"

"No, they moved to a condo after my brother and I graduated from college. I haven't been back since then."

Holding hands the whole way, they walked slowly down the sidewalk, admiring the displays of candy canes, blow-up Santas and snowmen, Christmas trees and angels, snowflakes, reindeer, ropes of lights, the Grinch, a house wrapped with lights in the shape of a ribbon and bow, the entire cast of *A Charlie Brown Christmas* on skates. If it was holiday related, some rendition of it was there, in glorious color and lit up like an airport landing strip. Hannah was happy to see that the basic outline of the display her father had created on their former home was the same, although the new owners had changed the lights from white to multicolored, added trees made of a spiral of lights to line the driveway, and put a sleigh and reindeer on the roof.

She told David stories about popping out of bushes in a glow-in-the-dark vest, angel wings, and halo to scare people walking by. Or standing still, as if part of the display, only to moan and move at an appropriate time. She also told him about the time the houses were vandalized and could tell from his expression he understood exactly how that had dented her belief in the spirit of the holiday.

After they'd evaluated every house on both sides of the street, they headed for the Horse Brass Pub.

Settled with a hot drink and their food ordered, David asked, "So, you in a better mood?"

"I have to admit you were right. I'd forgotten how beautiful the Lane is. It brought back a lot of memories. Thank you."

"I'd like to take credit for bringing back good times for you, but I had no idea you'd lived there. All I was aiming for was a few gasps of pleasure from you when you saw how spectacular the lights are."

She lifted her glass and clinked it against his. "Whatever your motive, the result was terrific. Cheers."

They sipped their drinks for a few moments before she said, "Tell me, I'm curious. Why are you such a fanatic about Christmas? It seems an odd thing for a nice Jewish guy to go all fanboy on."

He laughed. "I'm not sure I like being described that way. Makes me sound like I'm a groupie for a boy band."

Before she could apologize, he continued, "But to answer your question, I'm fascinated that, in all these different cultures, there are celebrations of light in one form or another at the darkest time of the year. Ancient Romans celebrated Saturnalia near the winter solstice. In India, it's Diwali; in Iran, a festival marking the triumph of light over dark. Stonehenge may even be a marker to show the winter solstice. The Swedes dress their daughters up as St. Lucia, with candles on their heads and—"

"That one I know quite personally. We had a Swedish neighbor who had no daughters. My mother wanted to celebrate the holiday with her, so we made St. Lucia buns to deliver to her on December thirteenth. My mother tried to make me wear an Advent wreath on my head with real candles. I refused. She was very annoyed that we put the candles on the tray with the coffee and buns. Not authentic enough, she said."

He laughed. "I'm beginning to understand more about your problem with the holidays. I don't think I'd want to have a head full of lighted candles either."

"The next year, I suggested we just make the buns and have coffee with her." The server interrupted with their dinners. When he had gone, Hannah said, "So, from Stonehenge to Peacock Lane. You really take this seriously, don't you? Is it the religious part that speaks to you?"

"Not really. You don't have to be religious to appreciate it. It's more like being part of a long tradition of reassurance—no matter how short the days are, or how dark the nights, the celebrations all promise the light will return."

"Well, that explains your fascination." She smiled. "I'm still not ready to get excited about the whole thing, but you have given me something to think about."

"My work here is done, then."

When they arrived at Hannah's home after their leisurely meal, she asked, "Want to come in and meet Sarah?"

"She's been appropriately warned this time?"

"I left her a note and asked her to be prepared for a visitor."

An introduction, a pot of coffee, and a half hour later, Hannah walked David back to his car. He stopped before stepping off the curb. "Thank you for going with me this evening."

"I should be thanking you. I felt like I'd gone home in some ways."

He circled her waist with his arms and drew her closer. "Good. Then we both got something we wanted. You got to remember your childhood. I got to spend another evening with you. And another chance to do this." He lowered his head until his mouth touched hers. She eagerly parted her lips and let him nibble at her lower lip before he stroked his tongue over hers. The shiver that raced through her had nothing to do with the chilly winter air and everything to do with what he was doing with his mouth and his hands, which were pressing her tight against the erection she could feel against her belly.

Changing the angle of his mouth on hers, he deepened the kiss, exploring her mouth, taking the oxygen from her lungs and sending all the moisture in her body south. It was what she'd been fantasizing about since the last time they'd been out. Only this time, it was better.

When he broke from the kiss, they were both breathing raggedly. He held her, kissing her hair, until their breathing got close to normal.

"The next time, I want ... " He stopped.

She tilted her head up and smiled at him.

He kissed her gently and released her. "I'll take that as agreement and hold you to it."

"Good night, David."

But as she turned to go back into her house he said, "Wait, we didn't figure out when 'next time' is. Next week must be busy for you. Do you work late every day the week before Christmas?"

"Most days."

"How about Friday? Are you working then?"

"No, I scheduled myself off."

"Friday it is." He stepped into the street and stopped. "Sorry, that was presumptuous of me. What I *meant* was, would you like to do something next Friday?"

Hannah laughed. "Is this the third and final attempt to change my mind about the holidays?"

"If that's how you want to look at it. Or you could just say I want to see you on Friday. Your call."

What *did* she want it to be? Oh, who was she trying to fool? After that kiss and its aftermath, there was no question. She wanted to spend more time with this man. And it had nothing to do with any bet. "Yes, I'd like to see you next Friday. It would give me something to look forward to after the week from Christmas Hell."

He winced. "I see I still have work to do on the whole holiday spirit thing, don't I?"

"As much as I'm enjoying the efforts you're making to change my mind—and believe me, I am—the dark side is still there every day at work, I'm afraid."

He grinned at her. "I love a challenge. And I never give up."

"Right. Persistence is your most annoying habit."

"You remember. Excellent. See you Friday."

Maybe it was the anticipation of seeing David again, or the shivers she got wondering if he meant what he'd intimated about "next time." Perhaps it was the enthusiasm of her staff when they discussed details of the SafePlace party they were planning. Maybe people were behaving better than usual when they shopped. Whatever it was, the week before Christmas wasn't nearly as stressful as she'd anticipated. In fact, by Wednesday she had to admit, to herself at least, that she was actually enjoying work, even if she was putting in long hours to pick up the slack for her ailing assistant manager. It wasn't an easy week, but it wasn't the week from hell she'd anticipated. Maybe David's enthusiasm was rubbing off on her after all.

Chapter 6

"You look beautiful. As always." David leaned in and dropped a quick kiss on her forehead. He wasn't much of an expert on women's clothing, but the navy dress she wore with brown boots and a wide belt that matched looked perfect on her. "Did you design this?" He indicated what she was wearing with a wave of his hand. "It's great."

"Yes, I did. Thanks. It's my take on the old standby shirtwaist dress. I wasn't sure what we were doing tonight, so I didn't know what to wear. But I figured this would work okay for everything, except maybe climbing a rock wall."

"I promise, if I ever decide to take you to a rock wall gym, I'll give you advance notice so you can dress for it."

She grabbed a coat from the hook on the wall by the door. He started to take it from her to help her put it on, but something behind her diverted his attention. "It looks like you're creating in there. Are you making some of your designs?"

Hannah turned. "Oh, you mean my sewing mess. I've been making doll clothes."

"Samples of your designs?"

"No, but that's a good idea. I might do that someday." She walked to the living room and picked up a finished dress. It was a halter-neck gown with a full, sweeping skirt in a blue and white chevron pattern. "It's for Hannah, too."

"Hannah, too?"

"My secret Santa girl from SafePlace. When I introduced myself as Hannah, she said she was 'Hannah, too,' so that's how I think of her. She asked for a doll. So I got her an American Girl doll, and I'm designing and making clothes for it. And I'm making one outfit for the doll's owner so they match."

"She'll be in heaven." He hesitated for a moment. "I'm not sure I should say this, but it seems to me you've caught a bad case of Christmas spirit." He shook his head, then kissed her gently to ward off a remark about his assumption.

"Hardly. This is my way of relaxing when I come home from work. And she deserves to have a nice present, don't you think?"

Both Hannahs deserved a good Christmas in his opinion, but he wasn't about to say that. So he merely commented, "From the looks of what you're doing, she'll have the best present ever. Although you are a little messy when you're creative. You obviously have a patient housemate."

"It drives her crazy when I do this, but she's in Seattle for a long weekend with her family, so I'm free to make a mess." She dropped her eyes and fussed with the collar of the coat she was holding. "So, back to tonight. What're we doing if we're not rock climbing?"

If he'd known she had an empty house for the weekend, he wouldn't have spent two hours trying to get his apartment into some sort of decent shape in the hopes of convincing her to go there after their date. However, from the almost embarrassed expression on her face, he thought it best not to let her know how happy it made him that she was thinking about what an empty house might mean for the end to their evening.

So he let her change the subject. He held up her coat, and she put it on. "If I told you the color you're wearing is perfect for what we're doing tonight, would it give you a clue?"

"There's a color theme?"

"Not a theme, exactly. But blue is an associated color, shall we say."

Her face scrunched up for a moment then broke into a smile. "Oh, Hanukkah. The color for Hanukkah is blue, isn't it?"

"Yup. We're going to a latke party, to eat way too many fried potato pancakes, play a silly game that becomes cutthroat in the circles I run in, and watch a bunch of candles burn down to nothing. Let's get going—they'll be waiting for us to get the party started."

The host and hostess for the latke party were college friends of David's, as were at least one of the partners in each of the other four couples. They'd been getting together for latkes one night of Hanukkah every year since college, and over time the group had grown to include spouses and eventually children. By now the group numbered six couples, four of them married, two who usually brought dates, and eight kids among them—totaling twenty people.

On the way to the event, David explained to Hannah they'd probably find everyone in the kitchen when they arrived—frying latkes, dishing up applesauce and sour cream, munching on cheese and crackers or vegetables and dip, pouring wine, or nagging about when the chocolate gelt would be parceled out for the dreidel tournament. Then, as soon as the final batch of latkes was ready, the candles in the menorah would be lit and the blessing given, after which the gorging on fried potato pancakes would take place.

It was all as David described it, down to the two after-dinner dreidel games. The children's game was noisy but well behaved. The adult version was, as advertised, cutthroat. There were accusations of cheating, threats of stealing the winnings of those who were ahead, and even one or two attempts at bribery. David was amused to see how competitive Hannah was and how quickly she fell into the banter and mock corruption of his friends.

The party broke up about eleven. Everyone urged Hannah to return the next year, with or without David, so they could win back the gelt she'd "stolen" from them because of her beginner's luck.

Every time he looked over at her as he drove her home, she was grinning. He was, too. It had been a great evening. She fit in with his friends. She was fun and funny, and he was falling for her so fast he knew he was in big trouble.

Finally he said, "I hope you had a good time."

"Of course I did. You have an amazing group of friends," she said. "You go a ways back with them, don't you?"

"First year of college. Eight of us in a comparative religion class decided to share holiday traditions with each other. Hanukkah fell early that year, so we made the latkes in the dorm on an illegal hotplate. They were terrible. I have no idea why anyone wanted to continue the tradition after that, but we did. Fortunately, we got better at making latkes. We rotate the venue from place to place each year, but everyone helps cook and clean up wherever we are."

He glanced over at her. "It was a good evening. And I'm not ready to end it yet. Are you?"

She scrunched over closer to him and put her hand on his leg. It was damned distracting. The feel of her hand, her vanilla scent that filled the car, and the sound of her soft laugh were building his anticipation about what might come next.

"I'm not ready to end it either. Are we going to my house or yours?" she asked, making the distraction even greater.

"Where would you rather go?"

"Weeelll," she said, deliberately dragging out her response, "I'm not sure. I guess it depends on what you have in mind."

He yanked on the steering wheel and pulled over to the curb. Without saying anything, he turned off the engine, unclipped his seatbelt, and slid toward her. He wrapped his arms around her and claimed her in a kiss he hoped would answer her question.

When he had thoroughly explored her mouth with his lips, tongue, and teeth, he eased off—but didn't release her. Instead he began kissing along her jawline until he reached her ear. "What I have in mind is to start like that," he whispered, "then, if it's okay with you, I'll unwrap you with all the attention I'd give to the best present I ever got."

He pulled back. "I'd start with this." Matching his actions to his words, he began opening the front of her coat, pushing it to the side so the front of her dress was exposed. "After I take care of those buttons, you'll take me to your bedroom and I'll work on these." He slipped his fingers behind the V at the neckline of her dress and undid the top button. His index finger strayed under the cup of a lacy-feeling bra to the soft breast underneath.

"When I've gotten your dress undone, I'll be able to see this lacy thing you're wearing. Doubt that I'll look at it too long, though. It would have to go." He brushed the palm of his hand over one breast and felt her nipple begin to pucker and harden. "Because I definitely want to kiss what's behind it."

He stopped playing with her clothes and drew her close again. Beginning at the swell of her breasts, now exposed, he kissed and licked his way up to the notch between her collarbones. "Then, after I get both our heart rates going, I'll find out if what else you wear under this dress is as lacy as your bra." His hand slid up her thigh to the edge of her panty leg. "Oh, good. I won't have to worry about getting you out of tights."

He could feel his own arousal increase as he continued to explore her hip, her belly, and the smooth bit of something silky that covered her sex. It was getting tougher to focus on seducing her with words when all he really wanted to do was get her into a bed someplace and finish the seduction with his body.

He heard her swallow—gulp, really—after she licked her lips a few times to moisten her mouth. "Go on," she said, "What else?"

"Then, I'll finish undressing you. It might be challenging to get all your clothes off because I imagine it'll be difficult to keep from kissing up your neck and finding your mouth again. Just like it is now."

She moaned as he demonstrated with a kiss what he meant. He wanted her so badly that he had a hard time keeping the kiss under control.

"After you're all undressed, I'll lay you down on your bed where I can see how beautiful you are. And I'll watch you while I take off what I'm wearing. Then I'll lay down beside you." He brushed his thumb over her mouth. "Do you like what I've got planned so far?" he asked.

After a shuddery intake of breath, she said, "Oh, yes. Very much." She ran her hands up his arms and circled his neck. "Keep going. What's next?"

"Well, now that we're both naked and lying in bed, it shouldn't be too difficult to imagine what's next, should it?"

"So we just let nature take its course."

"In a manner of speaking, I guess."

"Are you prepared?"

"Prepared?" He wasn't quite sure where she was headed with that question. Then he understood. "Oh, you mean do I have protection? Yes, I do."

"So, I was pretty much a sure thing for tonight?"

"You, sweetheart, are never a sure thing. But I'm an optimist."

"I think I like knowing that." She caressed his face. "So, all we have to do is decide where all this will be happening, is that right? Your place or mine?"

"Yours is closer."

It took longer to wipe off the steamed-up windshield than it did to drive to her house.

• • •

Hannah had never been seduced so effectively by words. David's kisses were potent—she'd been dreaming about them since the first time he kissed her—but his words were even more powerful. Oh, my God, his words. He had her wet and wanting with his description of what he wanted to do. If he could do that while they were fully dressed in his car, what would it be like when they were naked in her bed?

She was about to find out because they were at her house. She steadied herself with a few deep breaths before getting out of the car and walking up the steps to the door. Once there, however, her hand was so shaky she fumbled with the key, unable to get it into the lock until David covered her hand with his and guided her.

Inside the house, without saying anything more, he did exactly what he had described in the car—kissed her, took off her coat, then followed her into her bedroom, where he undressed them both, silently. The only sounds were their ragged breathing and the occasional involuntary gasp as his fingers brushed over her skin, already hypersensitive from the words he'd said.

Then they were lying side-by-side in her bed, facing each other, his hand caressing her body from her shoulder, down her arm, to her hip. The anticipation of what was next had ramped up her heartbeat and made breathing something she had to think about doing.

He finally broke the silence. "I've been dreaming about this for a week," he said. "I want to feel your skin, touch your breasts, kiss you right here." He dipped his head and made good on his words, his lips in the valley between her breasts. "You taste even better than I imagined. So sweet, so beautiful," he said when he raised his head.

She caressed the shoulder she'd wanted to touch since the first day she'd met him. "You're the one who's beautiful." She didn't think she'd ever seen such a toned and muscled body. He may have worked behind a desk, but he did something to keep himself in such good shape. Right now she didn't care what it was, only that he did it and she got to enjoy it.

He insinuated one leg between hers. "Hannah." Her name came out in a rush of breath, a whisper of desire. She ran a finger along his cheekbone and down his jawline, loving the scratchy feel of his day's worth of whiskers. He grabbed the finger and brought it to his lips, licking it, kissing it, then taking it into his mouth and sucking on it.

She felt the pull from her finger all the way down her body to her sex. It may have been the most erotic thing anyone had ever done to her. "Oh, God, David, you're killing me."

"You've been killing me all evening. All I could think about was this." He slid one hand into her hair and pulled her head toward him. His mouth was hot, hard, desperate for her. He dipped his tongue into her mouth, mating it with hers as she responded with equal passion.

Her body arched toward him. She could feel the hard length of his erection pressing against her belly, proof he wanted her just as much as she wanted him. But he seemed determined to take his time. Shifting on the bed, gently turning her on her back, he caressed one breast while he used his mouth and tongue to bring the nipple on the other to a pebbly point. Just when she thought she couldn't bear the intensity any longer, he switched and began his delightful torture on the other breast.

"Please," she pleaded. "I need … I want … "

"Tell me what you need, sweetheart. I'll do whatever you want me to."

"I need you. I want you."

"Like this?" He slid his hand down her torso and found the spot hidden in her sex where all the heat, all the moisture, all the want had pooled. As he massaged her clitoris with his thumb, he entered her—first with one finger, then two, finding another spot to caress. In what seemed like only seconds, the waves of an orgasm crashed over her, and the world contracted to just what David was doing to her. To the glorious way her body was responding to him.

"I love how ready you were for me. Love how beautiful you are when you come," he whispered as he held her, cushioning her descent from the heavenly feel of her climax. He waited until her breathing became more regular before moving between her legs. "I could touch and kiss you all night. I don't think I could ever get enough of you."

Her eyes locked on his. "But I want more than kissing and touching," she said.

He smiled. "Me, too." He reached under the pillow next to her where, she realized, he'd stashed a condom. "Help me put this on."

She wasn't sure who ripped open the packet. Maybe she did. Maybe he did. All she knew was it was opened, the condom pulled out, and he had been sheathed.

She needed him inside her. All of him. Inside. Now.

He was back between her legs, guiding himself into her, slowly, letting her adjust to the feel of him. She locked one leg around him, pressing her hips into his, eager to have him fill her. When he did, she stilled, wanting to savor the sensation. But her need for him wouldn't let her stay still for long. Restless to have him move inside her, she brought her other leg over his back and began to rock her hips.

Slowly at first, he moved in and out in a rhythm he matched with his tongue in her mouth. She could feel his rapid heartbeat against her own, the muscles in his shoulders and back tensing as he moved over her. Their bodies slid against each other on a slick of sweat as he drove into her harder, faster, deeper. They were flying together high over the city, where the air was cool and the oxygen rare. Where only a lucky few ever get to go.

Where he was taking her until she cried out his name, her body clenched around him, and they both found release.

• • •

Hannah was dancing to the music in her head as she ground beans and filled her coffee maker with water. Never in her thirty-two years had she felt so good the morning after a night spent with a man. Not that she had a huge cadre of men to compare him to, but David was an amazing lover. He seemed to care more about what she wanted than his own pleasure, although she was pretty sure from the two times they'd had sex the night before that he was as happy with their lovemaking as she was. As soon as the coffee was brewed, she was headed back to bed. Maybe they could make it three times.

Two strong arms pulling her against a muscled chest interrupted her musings. "There you are. I missed you," David said as he nuzzled the back of her neck. "I woke up, and you were gone. I knew you hadn't left because ... "

"Because it's my house?" She turned her head so she could see him. His bed hair and morning scruffy face were sexy as hell. Not to mention the feel of his body pressed against her back.

"Something like that," he said.

"I was making coffee to bring back to bed for us."

He turned her around and pulled her hard against him. "I'd rather have you in bed than coffee."

"You have me now, here."

"I'm not crazy about sex on the kitchen floor. It's not nearly as comfortable here as in your bed. As in any bed, for that matter."

"I've never had sex on the kitchen floor."

He sighed. "Okay, if you need to check it off your bucket list, I'm your man." He moved the bar stool from under the breakfast bar as if to make room for them on the floor.

His expression, some weird combination of resignation and arousal, made it difficult for her to keep a straight face. "It's okay. I'll take your word for how uncomfortable it is," she said.

The sound of the coffee maker expelling the last bit of water interrupted. "Coffee's done. Do you take milk or sugar?" she asked.

"Black. Thanks."

She filled two mugs. "Good. That makes it faster." Handing him one mug she said, "Now, about that more comfortable place to make love."

• • •

Thanks to the comfort of her bed, breakfast ran into lunch. After they'd showered and eaten, Hannah asked, "What's on your schedule for today?" hoping the answer was, "Nothing but you, sweetheart."

"You don't have a Christmas tree yet. I thought we'd go get one for you and decorate it together. Assuming you have lights and ornaments."

"Of course I do. I just don't always get around to dragging it all out."

"No wonder you don't feel the spirit. You don't have that fresh evergreen smell greeting you every time you walk into the living room. Or see the lights reflected in the ornaments. I bet you don't even have any Christmas music to listen to while we decorate."

"You're really into this, aren't you?" She rolled her eyes. "Yes, I have Christmas CDs. My mother made sure of it. I'm not sure where they are, but I can look."

"Tree first. I know this great tree farm where we can cut a fresh tree so it lasts all the way to Twelfth Night."

"Which branch of Judaism celebrates Twelfth Night?"

"That would be my late grandmother, the Episcopalian." He grabbed her coat from the hook by the door. "Enough questioning of my motives and religious upbringing. Unless you have a waterproof drop cloth, a saw, and some rope, we'll have to stop by my apartment."

"Do I want to know why you have a waterproof drop cloth, a saw, and rope? Are you some kind of serial killer?"

"You've been watching too many crime shows."

• • •

Their perfect Friday evening segued into an even more perfect Saturday, which ended with a dinner they cooked together and another night of sweet explorations in bed. Hannah had to admit—to herself, if not yet to David—that cutting down a cute little tree and decorating it with him while listening to Christmas CDs had been fun. It made her feel like she was part of the season in a way she hadn't felt since she was a kid. But how could it not? He was so full of enthusiasm it was hard to resist.

On Sunday, Hannah was scheduled to work and David had to meet his sister to pick up a birthday gift for his niece. They parted with a lingering kiss.

After work that evening, as she finished up hand sewing the doll clothes for Hannah, too, and wrapped a Harry Potter Lego set for her other secret Santa, the younger Hannah's little brother, she realized how eagerly she was looking forward to the party at SafePlace. It was partly because she'd see David, but she also had to acknowledge she wanted to be part of the celebration with the kids. Wanted to see the expression on Hannah, too's face when she opened her gifts.

She also had to admit she was feeling the urge to bake snickerdoodles and gingerbread men. Maybe even take a plate of them to SafePlace during her lunch break to surprise David. Was it possible he *had* begun to convince her that there was something good in celebrating the season? Should she give in and admit he was close to winning the bet? She wasn't quite ready to do that, but decorating a tree and baking cookies were surely steps in that direction.

Chapter 7

Hannah almost didn't make it out of her office on Tuesday to deliver the cookies she'd made for David. Between helping her staff take care of people who'd put off shopping and were now racing through the store in a panic, and nailing down the last-minute details of the party at SafePlace, she had barely a moment to breathe. But finally, she squeezed out fifteen minutes to make her delivery. David's assistant wasn't around when she got to his office, but his door was open and she could see he was in.

He was on the phone, his back to her. She paused outside the door, not wanting to interrupt.

"Look," he was saying. "I know I promised I'd take care of her, but I had no idea what it would entail. She requires one hell of a lot of attention."

There was a pause, as he apparently listened to whoever was on the other end of the call.

He laughed. "I know. I know. I owe you. But when you asked me this favor, I thought it would be a lot easier than it turned out to be. She's cute in her puppy dog way, but you're asking a lot by leaving her to my tender mercies."

Another pause.

"Like I said, she's really high maintenance. I'm looking forward to Christmas being over and getting her out of my hair." He paused for a response, then laughed again. "I just mean I'll have my life back. I have other plans, you know, for how I want to spend my free time."

Who was David talking to? Who was he talking about? Who did he owe ... ? A poisonous answer slithered its way into her mind. *No, it couldn't be. Could it? He didn't mean ... Did he?*

Not wanting to hear any more, Hannah backed away from the door as quietly as she could. Once in the hall, she took off at a run, anxious to get out of the building before anyone saw her. Her head hurt. Her chest was tight. She had to get away.

A block later, she realized she was still clutching the paper plate piled with David's cookies. A panhandling homeless woman with a small child caught her eye. Even the little boy's profuse thanks for the unexpected gift weren't enough to ease the pain in her head.

Slipping into a Starbucks, she sat in the corner with an eggnog latte and tried to sort out what she had just overheard.

First, she'd heard the man who professed to love Christmas say he wanted the holiday over and done with so he could get his life back. Second, he'd undertaken a responsibility at the request of someone he owed a favor to. Third, he'd been taking care of someone—not just *someone*—a woman, who demanded a lot of attention.

Who would be out of his life—out of his hair—after Christmas? The answer seemed obvious. With the party over, *she* would be. But did he really think of her as cute in a puppy dog way? Or as high maintenance?

No matter how she parsed the sentences, there was only one answer she could come up with. He'd paid attention to her because he promised Mr. Austin he would. Mr. Austin, who had done so much for SafePlace. But why would Simon Austin ask that favor of David? Granted, there had been quite a few complaints sent to corporate from dissatisfied customers over the past few weeks, but had there been so many that he was worried about her management of his store?

Or was he concerned she'd taken on more than she could handle, with Angie gone and the SafePlace campaign to organize? He'd seemed worried about it that first meeting in her office. Had he asked David to step in and help? Maybe he had. David had offered to help at almost every turn, hadn't he? Was that just to please Mr. Austin?

Crap. Why hadn't she seen it before? David wasn't interested in her. He was just another man trying to advance his career by using her, doing what had been asked of him because he wanted the money Simon Austin could contribute to SafePlace. She'd thrown herself at David like a fool, and because he wasn't crazy, he'd caught what was so eagerly pitched. Just because he headed a program that helped kids and abused women didn't mean he was any different than any other guy.

Damn. Damn. Damn. David had suckered her into caring about Christmas—about *him*—when he wasn't much better than the-dipshit-whose-name-was-forbidden. She'd been right all along. Christmas spirit was bullshit, nothing more than an excuse to use people to get what you wanted for yourself.

She finished her coffee, crumpled the cup, and tossed it into the trash. She didn't need David Shay's help to get through Christmas. And she'd make sure Mr. Austin knew it before the week was over. As for David—she'd give him what he wanted. After this week, she'd be out of his life.

She shut down the voice in her head asking if she was sure that was what *she* wanted, and went back to her store.

• • •

Hannah threw herself into her work, putting in extra-long days, taking over the hours of parents on staff who needed flexibility to attend their kids' school programs, and making sure she was slated to be there the very busy day after Christmas and the following weekend. She even canceled her time off over New Year's. She'd show Mr. Austin and everyone else she could do everything that had to be done, and do it well.

The store closed at four on Christmas Eve, and most of the staff eagerly walked to SafePlace for the two-hour party they'd all done so much to organize. Mandy and one other staffer had spent the better part of the afternoon there, directing the caterers and helping SafePlace staff arrange tables and chairs. Hannah was the only person reluctant to go. She knew she couldn't escape David in person as easily as she'd avoided his phone calls and texts over the past few days, messages that had started out sweet and sexy and had become progressively more hurt and confused as she continued to ignore them.

The party was a roaring success. The Santa they'd hired was amazing. The kids put on a wonderful program explaining the significance of the holidays featured in their decorations. The food was delicious. The face painting, balloon animals, and photo booth were hits.

The best part, for Hannah, was it was so crowded she'd been able to get away with only a superficial greeting to David when she arrived. She hadn't been able to avoid seeing the hurt look in his eyes, but she'd steeled herself to ignore it.

She looked around for Hannah, too, but the little girl found her first.

"Hannah One, you were right! Santa knew where I was and brought me the most beautiful doll in the world. Her name's Isabelle, she has blonde hair just like me, and she came with lots of clothes. I even got a shirt like one of hers." The little girl grabbed the adult Hannah's hand. "Come see her."

Hannah allowed herself to be dragged over to a table where a tired-looking woman and a small boy were sitting. "Mommy, this is Hannah One. She told Santa where George and I were so he could find us."

The woman put out her hand. "I'm Lisa, and I'm so happy to meet you. My Hannah talks about you all the time. You and David are her two favorite people in the world right now." She turned to her children. "Hannah, George, would you go get us two cups of juice and some cookies?" The children tore off to the food table.

"I wanted a chance to say thank you in private. You have no idea how much it meant to my daughter when you told her you'd take care of Santa finding her. She was worried, more for her brother than for herself, I think, but she believed you when you reassured her. And David told me you designed and made all those clothes for Hannah's doll. They're beautiful. You're very talented."

Hannah ducked her head, embarrassed at the compliments. "Thank you. I had a wonderful time making them."

The children returned, carefully carrying two paper cups of juice and a plateful of cookies. "We got one of each kind, Mommy, because we weren't sure what you wanted," Hannah said.

George put the plate on the table. "Can I go back to building Hogwarts now?"

"As long as you keep it all in the box. You don't want to lose any of the pieces before we even leave the party."

Hannah was aware of David before she saw or heard him. She swore her hair stood on end, her breath caught, her heartbeat increased. It must have been the smell of his cologne or something that set her body off, but whatever it was, she knew without turning around that David Shay was standing behind her.

"Sorry to interrupt, Lisa, but I'd like to talk to Hannah for a minute," he said.

Without turning around, she asked, "Is there a problem with something?"

"Let's talk privately." He took Hannah by the elbow, leaving her no option unless she wanted to make a scene, and led her to an empty classroom. "What's with the cold shoulder?"

"I don't know what you mean."

"You've been ignoring my texts and phone calls. You barely spoke to me when you got here. What did I do that pissed you off?"

"I've been busy." She made as if to leave, but he grabbed her arm.

"Maybe we should—"

Shaking off his hand, she said, "Maybe we should just let it go. You won't have to deal with me after today."

"Won't have to … ? What the hell does that mean?"

"Just what I said." She made it to the door and looked out. "There's Mr. Austin. I need to make sure things have been done to his satisfaction." Not letting David detain her any longer, she escaped back into the crowd.

"Mr. Austin!" Eager to get away from David, Hannah almost shouted to get her boss's attention.

He turned abruptly. "Hannah. There you are. I've been looking for you to tell you what a wonderful job you and your staff did with the party."

"I'm glad you're happy."

"I know it added more to an already busy season for you, but I was confident you were up to it."

"You seemed concerned about that when we first talked."

"Concerned? About you? Never. There's nothing I can throw at you that you can't handle." He grinned at her. "Which leads me to the second reason I wanted to talk to you. I'm about to do a major overhaul of all the stores, and I need a project manager working with me in corporate to oversee it." He put his hand on her shoulder. "Interested in the job?"

"Me? Working with you in corporate? Of course I'm interested. I'm honored you have that much confidence in me."

"I've always had confidence in you. You can do anything. You already do everything, as far as I can tell. Which brings me to the last thing I want to say. One of Santa's helpers told me you're quite a good clothing designer. And I was impressed by what you made for your secret Santa present. How would you like to meet with one of our clothing manufacturers to see if we can get him interested in producing your line for my stores?"

Hannah didn't answer right away. Couldn't answer because she was afraid she'd burst into tears or dissolve into nervous giggles. Finally, after she took a deep breath, she said, "I'm overwhelmed."

"Thank David for that last idea. He was the one who urged me to look at your work."

"David? I thought—"

"He's quite a fan, you know." Mr. Austin smiled. "I think in more than a professional way, but that's for you to sort out between the two of you."

"Oh, I'm sure not. Like he told you over the phone, he'll be happy to get on with his life now that he doesn't have to worry about working with me on this party."

"I haven't talked to David on the phone in weeks. We have lunch once a week and do all our business there."

"But I heard him."

"Whatever you heard, you misunderstood." He looked over Hannah's shoulder. "I just got the signal that I'm expected at the podium for my little speech. Let's get together after the first of the year and work out your transition to corporate." He gave Hannah a pat on the back. "And merry Christmas."

"Thank you, Mr. Austin. The same to you."

Hannah stood, dazed, while her boss wrapped the party up and her staff came by to wish her Merry Christmas. But when she saw David headed toward her, a determined look on his face, she bolted. She couldn't face him. Not until she figured out how to bluster her way out of being rude to him about that conversation she'd overheard and still hadn't figured out.

Chapter 8

"So, what you're telling me is your party was a success, you got an offer of a huge promotion, and the guy you've fallen for got you a shot at having your clothing designs considered for production—geesh, are there any more wishes left in the magic lamp you found, and can I have them?" Sarah asked.

"Sarah, you're not listening to me. He wants me out of his hair. He has other plans for his life." Hannah was pacing the floor in front of her housemate.

"So, we're focusing on the David Shay part of this story, not the job or the clothing line. Gotcha. Okay. What I hear is you trying to hold onto an idea you've got stuck in your head about a conversation you apparently misunderstood."

"But it was so clear when I heard it."

"Did you ask David about it?"

"Of course not. It was too embarrassing."

"But not embarrassing to have your boss tell you David's interested in you while you try to get him to say he dissed you."

Hannah stopped pacing and looked up at the ceiling. "Oh, crap. You're right. I screwed up. Now I'll have to get up the courage to face David and ask him to explain. Probably even apologize. But I have no idea what to say."

There was a knock at the door. Sarah looked through the security peephole and said, "Better figure it out quickly. He's here." She opened the door. "Hi, David. Come on in. I hear the party was a success."

David entered and stared across the room at Hannah. "It went well, yes."

No one said anything more for a few moments.

"Well," Sarah said, "I think I hear my television calling me. It's upstairs, if anyone's interested. Where I'll be. With the door closed. And the TV on at high volume so I won't be able to hear anything but the stupid program I'm watching. In case anyone cares. Which I doubt." She left her roommate and their visitor standing on opposite sides of the room, silent and staring.

Hannah finally spoke. "Shouldn't you be cleaning up after the party? Or something?"

"My staff said they'd take care of it. I told them we had a conversation to finish."

She groaned. "Oh, God, is there anyone who doesn't know about this?"

"I'm not sure *I* know about this. Whatever it is. But if you'll tell me, maybe I can try and make it right."

She looked at the floor, her eyes shut, and muttered, "I heard what you said on the phone."

He came closer. "You're whispering. Say again."

She raised her head and her voice. "I heard what you said on the phone."

"What I said? When?"

"Tuesday. Around lunchtime. When I brought some Christmas cookies to your office for you. I heard you say—"

"You brought me Christmas cookies? I never got them." He was close enough to put his hands on her shoulders, but she shook them off when he tried.

"That's not the point."

"Then tell me what the point is."

"I heard you say I was cute like a puppy dog, but I was high maintenance and you could hardly wait to get rid of me so you could get your life back."

"Puppy dog? You thought I called you a puppy dog?" He struggled to suppress a smile and failed. In fact, the smile progressed rapidly to a grin and then a laugh.

"You think it's funny I heard you call me that? Heard what you really think of me? I thought you were talking to Mr. Austin, but he denied it. I don't know who you were talking to, but it hurt."

David fumbled in his jacket pocket and pulled out his phone. He touched the screen, then swiped it a couple times without saying anything.

Hannah's embarrassment was quickly being replaced with anger. "You're not even denying it? You're just laughing at me and playing with your phone?"

He turned the phone around so she could see the screen.

She glanced at the image—of a dog. "What's that got to do with it?"

"Everything. Remember how on Sunday I had to go meet my sister about a present for my niece? Well, here's the present—a Jack Russell puppy. My sister picked her up from the breeder on Sunday, but needed someplace to stash her until the birthday party. The puppy has been my roommate since then. Jack Russells are notorious for needing a lot of attention, it turns out. You overheard me complaining to my sister that if I'd known that, I might have said no, even though she plays on my sympathy all the time."

"But you said you could hardly wait until Christmas was over. How can you love Christmas but want it over with?"

"This year, it's easy. In a wonderful ironic twist, my nice, observant Jewish sister produced her daughter on Christmas Day ten years ago."

"Oh."

"*Oh* is all you have to say?"

"Well, maybe, I'm sorry."

"*Maybe* you're sorry? Oh, sweetheart, you can do better than that." By this time, he had Hannah in his arms and was kissing her forehead, cheeks, and nose between words. She didn't resist.

"Okay, I'm definitely sorry. I was sure what I heard was about me. And so disappointed because you said you wanted Christmas over with. Just when I'd—"

"Just when you'd begun to think you could enjoy the season?" This time the kiss landed on her mouth, with all the tenderness and affection she could have wanted.

Then he abruptly pulled his head back. "Wait. Let's get back to the cookies. I didn't know Scrooge could bake. And where are they?"

"I gave them to a homeless woman and her son."

"You did a good deed in the spirit of the season even when you were pissed off! Wow. I'm better at this *Christmas Carol* stuff than I thought. But you owe me cookies." He touched his thumb to her lower lip. "And an admission that you had a good time making doll clothes for Hannah ... "

She nibbled on his thumb. "And I owe you a thank-you for being the elf who told Mr. Austin about my clothing designs. He's going to introduce me to one of our manufacturers to see if he'd be interested in producing my line for the stores."

"So, let me see—you got to relive some Christmas happiness from your childhood on Peacock Lane, you gave a little girl the best Christmas of her life, you baked Christmas cookies and cleaned up at dreidel, and Santa Austin is making your dreams come true. Does that mean ... ?"

"It means I give up. I can't fight anymore. I loved Christmas this year. I didn't even mind the last-minute Christmas rush at the store. You've won the bet."

"Yeah, I know I have. I knew I'd win the first time I saw you with Hannah, too. But you realize I have no intention of waiting 'til New Year's for the kiss I won, don't you?"

"I was hoping you'd collect tonight."

"I think I can make that wish come true, too."

More from This Author
(From *Unmasking Love* by Peggy Bird)

"Do you have a minute, Greer?"

Greer Payne looked up from the boring deposition she was reviewing for a fellow deputy D.A. and smiled hopefully at Multnomah County District Attorney Jeff Wyatt, her boss. "I always have time for you, Jeff. Especially if you have something juicy for me to work on."

Her smile faded when he carefully closed the door without responding or smiling back. "The FBI report came back on the Dreier matter and I wanted to talk to you about it."

The few traces of hope that remained in her soul disappeared. "Have a seat. Can I get you coffee or something? Oh, wait, you've probably already had your coffee, haven't you? Or have you?" She knew she was babbling but couldn't seem to shut up.

"I'm fine, thanks. Don't bother. I won't be here long." He dropped a file folder on her desk. "I've excerpted the pieces of the report and the grand jury indictments I thought relevant for you to see. In a nutshell, the FBI and the grand jury concluded you didn't do anything illegal and weren't responsible for the leaks about the interagency task force. Dreier and the Russian mobsters he was working with got their information from another source."

"Can you tell me who the source was?"

"I don't think that's relevant. Suffice it to say, they determined it wasn't you."

What little pride Greer still had bubbled to the surface. "Of course it wasn't me. I might have dated the guy, but I wasn't stupid or careless enough to give him information about what was going on in this office."

"You weren't stupid—aren't stupid. But your judgment in continuing to be associated with someone everyone in the legal community knew skated close to the edge of the law ..."

She waved off the end of the sentence she had heard—and read—too many times in the past four months since her former lover had been arrested on charges of industrial espionage, kidnapping of a deputy D.A., and accessory to several murders. "I'll regret that lapse in judgment to the end of my life, believe me." She picked up the file folder he'd left on her desk. "Thank you for bringing this to me personally."

"Of course." Jeff turned to leave, then stopped and faced her again. "One more thing. For the time being, and for I'm not sure how long, what happened is going to be, shall we say, career-limiting for you. I'll be keeping you under wraps so some journalist doesn't revive what happened a few months ago when you're prosecuting a case and contaminate it with bad press. That means you're going to be stuck in the office doing some pretty low-key tasks. Do you think you can handle that?"

"Do I have a choice?"

"Not if you want to continue working here, you don't."

"Then that's the answer, isn't it?"

He stared at her intently. "I don't understand what you mean by that, exactly, but I'm sure you'll let me know." He left, quietly closing the door behind him.

Greer sat stunned, not moving for what seemed like an hour but was probably only five minutes. In spite of her hopes, her exile to the Siberia of dull and unrewarding paperwork while she waited to have her name cleared wasn't going to end any time soon. It apparently didn't help that she was innocent. The downward slide of her reputation as one of the best legal minds in the D.A.'s office wasn't going to be reversed any time soon. All that was left was to answer the question Jeff asked: could she handle being pushed to the sidelines professionally for an unknown period of time because of a bad decision in her personal life?

And if she couldn't, what were her other choices? Quit the D.A.'s office for a private practice in Portland? That wasn't likely to work out. Her association with her discredited boyfriend would follow her. So ... what, then? Leave Portland? That might not be a bad idea. Maybe she would be better off someplace where no one had ever heard of Paul Dreier, the Russian mob, or her taste in men. She had friends and family in California. Perhaps it was time to head south, back where she came from, to lick her wounds and regroup. Maybe, in fact, it was time for Greer Payne to simply disappear.

Because she sure as hell wasn't going to be happy sitting meekly in her office day after day watching everyone else get the good cases while she was assigned as pooper-scooper for the prize ponies in the parade.

She rummaged through her messenger bag for the business card the real estate agent had left when she'd come to see if Greer was interested in selling her condo. She picked up the phone, punched in the number and, when the call was answered, said, "Hi, this is Greer Payne. About that offer on my condo ..."

• • •

A month later, Greer was roaring south on I-5 at a speed that would guarantee her one hell of a ticket if she was pulled over. But she didn't care. She was headed for California, and the faster she put this wretched state in her rearview mirror the happier she'd be. The landscape whizzed past her as, gradually, the green farms and forests of Oregon's Willamette Valley and Siskiyou Mountains began to turn to the yellow-brown hills more like the Golden State's scenery. She was almost there. She swore she could even smell California, it was that close. Excitement began to replace the tension and anger she'd been carrying around for months.

But less than thirty miles from the border, she heard a peculiar noise. It wasn't like any road noise she'd ever heard. It sounded more like it came from someplace inside the car. Panicked at first, she calmed down as it seemed to disappear when a new song started on her iPod. Relieved, she kept going. It had probably just been some odd instrumentation in the R & B she had blasting at decibel levels likely to make her deaf before the trip was over.

However, ten miles later she heard the noise again as she pulled away from a pit stop near Ashland, where she'd gotten one last tank of gas someone else had to pump. It was definitely the car, not her music.

Unwilling to believe her beloved Lexus would abandon her as most of her colleagues in Portland had, she ignored what she heard and turned toward the I-5 entrance ramp. But as she accelerated to get onto the freeway there was another weird noise, the car refused to shift into a higher gear, and the check engine light went on. She pulled over to the side of the on ramp and stopped. All she could think to do was what she did with a balky computer—she turned the ignition off, waited a few seconds, and turned it back on. The engine revved but the car didn't move. No matter what she tried, it refused to budge from its new home on the side of the road.

Fuck. One more desertion.

The tow truck arrived half an hour later, but the man from the garage couldn't get the car going either. The best he could do was offer her a ride into town after he loaded her car onto his truck. She was stuck for what he warned might be several days until they could figure out what was wrong.

She wanted to scream. So close to escaping, yet so far from succeeding. Although she shouldn't have been surprised. Being stranded in Ashland with a broken-down car went along with everything else that had gone wrong lately. There was no point in being disappointed. She just had to suck it up and live with it.

Yeah. Right. If she could convince herself to be calm about this, she'd be eligible for sainthood.

• • •

The room the woman at the visitor's center found for her was in a remodeled fifties motel that had been turned into a comfortable and beautifully appointed place to stay. The owners lived on site and had been alerted to her situation before she arrived.

"You poor thing," the woman at the front desk said as Greer filled out the registration information. "Car trouble is such a pain." She looked down at the paperwork in front of her. "Oops. Sorry. With your last name, I guess we don't make pain jokes."

Greer smiled for the first time in quite a few hours. "It's okay. I'm used to it."

"Well, the bright side of this is you'll have a chance to see Ashland. Ever been here before?"

"Yeah. Came up from California to the Shakespeare Festival every summer for years."

The woman looked at the registration form again. "You gave an Oregon address."

"I've been living in Portland for a few years, but I'm moving back to California. The visits were when I was a kid. Came here with my mother and sisters."

"If you haven't been here in a while, you might find a few things have changed. Why don't you take a walk around while we get your room ready? You can leave your luggage here. It'll be safe."

With nothing better to do until she could hole up in her motel room for the night, Greer wandered back toward town. The woman at the motel was right—some things had changed. Her mother's favorite French restaurant was gone, replaced by a newer, trendier eating establishment. The store where her older sister had always found clothes she liked was now a convenience store. And there was a new indoor theater added to the outdoor Elizabethan theater and the Bowmer indoor space.

But the bones of the town were the same. Ashland still had the comfortable feel of a small town that just happened to have at its core a world-class theater company.

It was also very much Oregon, as Greer found out when she ordered a late lunch at a restaurant near Lithia Park. In a manner usually reserved for explaining the provenance of a valuable painting or a special bottle of wine, her server assured her that the chicken salad on field greens she ordered was local and free-range.

After lunch she cruised through a few clothing stores where there were end-of-season sales going on. She hadn't planned on spending money on clothes, as she faced the probability of a large car repair bill and had no job waiting for her in California. But when one shop owner lowered the price of a green dress that matched the color of Greer's eyes and that the woman said was meant for her, Greer had given in. How could she resist when the owner had been so accommodating

A couple more pleasant encounters with the shop owners and residents of Ashland later, Greer realized, as she walked back to her motel, that for the first time in months she was beginning to feel relaxed—in spite of the car breakdown, the unknown cost of repairs, and the forced change of plans. Her good mood might be a reaction to the beautiful autumn day—she was walking ankle-deep in colorful fallen leaves past shop windows that were beginning to be dressed for Halloween. The air was crisp and clean, the sun warm on her face.

Or maybe it wasn't the warmth of the sun that had relaxed her, but the warmth of the people she'd met. For a town overrun with tourists for most of the year, Ashland was remarkably friendly. *Maybe*, she thought, *it wouldn't be so bad to be stuck here for a few days. I can hang out, relax, get my car repaired, and be back on the road in a day or two feeling a little less stressed and ready to face whatever's next.*

That thought held until the next morning when she called the garage. The conversation started with the mechanic saying, "We've discovered what's wrong with your car, Ms. Payne."

"Great. How much will it cost, and how long will it take to fix it?"

"Minimum cost is a couple thousand dollars. And it'll take four or five days, maybe longer, to get it repaired."

"Ouch. What costs that much and takes so long?"

"Your transmission's shot. And, unless we can find one in a shop nearby, we have to order a new one. It'll take a few days to get here. I'm sorry I don't have better news for you."

"How's it shipped, slow boat from Tokyo?"

The mechanic snorted. "If we need to order it, it'll be FedEx from Canada, actually. We'll start tracking a tranny down as soon as you come in and sign a work order."

With no other choice, Greer signed the papers, extended her stay at the motel, and began what felt like a hospital vigil waiting for her sick car to come through surgery.

By day five, with no end to her stay in sight, Greer was about out of patience. She was also out of things to divert her from worrying about the cost of this forced "vacation." The charm of having the Starbucks barista know what she would order as soon as she walked in every morning had worn off. As had the welcome she got from the employees at Bloomsbury Books, all of whom greeted her by name each time she picked up the morning paper.

Then just when she thought nothing good could possibly happen to her ever again, her luck turned.

She was settled at a table with her paper in Brothers', her favorite breakfast place, when she overhead a conversation between two men she'd often seen in Starbucks and around town. She'd figured out they were attorneys from the conversations she'd heard before and had often eavesdropped just to hear the professional chitchat they engaged in—the kind of banter between legal colleagues she missed. Today, however, it was more than just chitchat.

"Did you see in the paper that Wilson Montgomery's moving to Arizona?" the younger man asked.

"No, that's a surprise. I thought he'd be in the legislature until he was wheeled out of the House chamber on a gurney." His companion laughed.

"Apparently not. He's closing his law practice, selling his house, and leaving town. Wants to be in a warmer climate, I guess."

"Sorry to lose him. I don't always agree with his politics, but he knows more about consumer fraud than any other lawyer for three counties. No one else has his expertise. We'll miss that."

Consumer fraud? They were talking about *her* area of expertise. She'd prosecuted more cases like that than all the rest of the deputies in Jeff's office combined. She leaned over and interrupted them. "Excuse me for eavesdropping, but I couldn't help hearing your conversation. Are you saying there might be a need in town for a lawyer with consumer fraud experience?"

"Yeah, you know one?" the younger man asked.

"I may," she replied.

"If you do, there's a law practice just begging to be taken over."

"Who would I contact? I mean, if I knew someone, a friend maybe, who was interested."

The older man cocked his head and smirked. "If you're seriously interested—or your *friend* is—call Wilson Montgomery." He pulled a business card out of his jacket pocket and wrote something on the back of it. "Here's the phone number." He started to hand it to her then pulled it back. "You a lawyer?"

"Yes, I am."

"Member of the Oregon bar?"

"Yup."

"Interesting. Never recruited an attorney in a restaurant before."

"You may still not have."

He barked out a laugh. "Yeah, right." Handing her the business card he said, "I'm Jim Foster. This is George Ross. And you're …?"

"Julie Payne."

She'd replied without thinking and was so stunned at her response that she was sure she looked relieved when the man merely said, "Nice to meet you, Julie Payne. Hope we see you again." She said nothing more as the two of them rose from their table and left after a brief conversation with the restaurant owner.

Julie Payne? Where the hell had that come from? Well, okay. She knew where it had come from. But she sure didn't know *why* it had come out in the course of that particular conversation. On the drive from Portland, she'd toyed with the idea of killing off Greer Payne and resurrecting her childhood name, but she hadn't thought more about it since she'd been in town.

Her whole, legal birth name was Juliet Greerson Payne. Her family called her Juliet, a name she'd dumped in high school when she'd gotten tired of *Romeo and Juliet* jokes. She'd chosen Greer, a version of her middle name, which was the family name of her beloved grandparents. No one in her family ever called her Greer, but everyone else had, from high school on.

This morning, she'd changed all that by introducing herself as Julie. She could be Julie if she stayed in Ashland. If she had the nerve to follow up on that conversation and call the guy who was leaving town.

It had some appeal. God knows she liked the feel of the town. She'd been made to feel at home by everyone she'd met, from the tow truck driver up to and including the two lawyers she'd just talked to, since the first moment she'd arrived in town. It wasn't as if she knew what her plans were when she got to California. She'd done some online job searching while she'd been hanging around waiting for her car, but she hadn't found anything that had caught her fancy. Not the way the conversation she'd just overheard had.

Even if she found something right away in California, she'd have limited usefulness as a practicing attorney until the following year when she could take the bar exam. She'd be able to get right to work in Oregon, where she was already a member of the bar.

With the obscene amount of money she'd gotten from the sale of her overpriced waterfront condo in Portland and what she knew she could get out of her Public Employees Retirement System account, she could probably buy into an existing law practice as well as purchase a house in Ashland. Who knew what she could buy in the expensive California market?

Even changing her name wouldn't be a problem—her college and law school diplomas as well as her bar membership, hell, even the credit card she'd used to check into her motel, were all in her full, legal name.

A new job. A new life. Wasn't that what she'd been running to? She might be able to have it all by staying right where she was. All she had to do was make a phone call and see what was out there. She looked at the business card in her hand and made a decision. She'd do it. Julie Payne would make that call. The hell with Greer and the problems she'd left behind in Portland.

For more great novels from Peggy Bird, check out these titles:

A Holiday for Love series:

Sparked by Love

Praise for *Sparked by Love:*

"With lies and hidden agendas, you have to wait and see till the very end for all the pieces to fall together!"—Chicks That Read

"A warm, fuzzy romance read. Leo and Shannon are just so sweet together. There is plenty of steam as well. Very enjoyable read for romance lovers."—Wilovebooks, 4 stars

"This book had the Triple 'S' factor for me: short, sweet and sexy . . . a wonderful book."—Red's Hot Reads, 4 stars

"This was my first time reading Peggy Bird. I was pleasantly surprised by not only her writing style, which was very engaging and flowed, but also her characters."—Book Nerd, 4 stars

Second Chances series:

Beginning Again

Praise for *Beginning Again*:

"Both Liz and Collins are great characters. Liz is not a bitter middle aged woman, but instead a very strong and brave lady. I really enjoyed *Beginning Again* because it was an easy read that made my gray autumn day a little bit less gray."—Long & Short Reviews

Loving Again

Together Again

Praise for *Together Again*:

"…a very enjoyable romance. I loved the main characters and the great writing. I always admire strong, independent women, so if you also enjoy those qualities in a heroine, and enjoy a well-written romance, I recommend this one."—Night Owl Reviews

Trusting Again

Praise for *Trusting Again*:

"The book moves along at a nice pace and the characters are believable and realistic. It is a well-written story with a wonderful ending!"—Harlequin Junkie

Believing Again

Falling Again

Printed in the United States
By Bookmasters